Finding

A Novelette Written By:
Kiara Jonai'

Finding Solace
A Novelette Written By:
Kiara Jonai'

Disclaimer:

This work of fiction contains some explicit sexual and is only intended for mature readers. This piece also contains some explicit adult language, occurrences, situations, and decisions.

Enjoy!

Synopsis

Amira Wright is one of the top lawyers at Wright & Curtis Law Firm; a law firm owned by her family. Her dad was an attorney, her mom was an attorney, and her sisters were both attorneys, so she ended up being an attorney as well. She always had the finer things in life, as long as she lived the life her parents wanted her to live. She lacked a social life and love life, all because she allowed her parents to dictate that as well. Her sisters were married; she was the last one left. What happens when she stumbles across an unlikely love opposite of what her parents would "allow"? Will she finally find solace and live her own life? And will this unlikely love bring her more than she bargained for?

Markell Davis, former felon, who is now taking the right path for a better life for he and his daughter. What happens when he's set up for a crime he didn't commit? Because of his past he must get the best lawyer his money could buy. What are the odds of him he finding love on the way? Will mishaps bring him back to his old ways despite his newfound happiness and better ways?

Chapter One-Amira

Another day, another dollar. Today was like any other day. Waking up at 5:30 every morning getting ready for a day at work. I decided to get cute today, don't know why. I'm not interested in any of the men my parents try to set me up with, especially any colleagues at work. I'm so over those over entitled men that work at the firm.

I am currently one of the most successful lawyers in Louisiana and one of the youngest as well. I'm very proud of myself nevertheless, however I know there's so much more to life for me.

Before heading to the firm, I headed to the coffee shop near my condo called "Jonai's". I've been coming here every morning before work for as long as I could remember. It's sort of a routine.

"Good morning Amira. Getting your usual this morning?" the barista Ms. Betty asked.

"Yes ma'am. Also, a sausage biscuit please." I said.

"You got it babe"

I began scrolling through my phone that is never popping. I had one message from Kyle and another from my sister. Kyle is my ex-boyfriend. He's also an attorney, one my parents set me up with. Things were actually okay for a while. It was going well until I caught him sleeping with his assistant. My mom begged me to forgive him. I forgave him, but I wouldn't forget. Now he is the father of her two kids, one that was conceived while he and I were together.

After that, I was over these men my parents picked out. They may have been prolific in the limelight but were dogs under the radar.

Ms. Betty handed my latte and I was on my way to work.

Walking in the firm and all you could hear was light classical music playing, phones ringing, fax machines, and people typing. I was snapped out of my thoughts by my legal assistant, who happens to be my best friend.

"Morning bestie! Boy do I have some tea for you?" She rambled while she followed me to my office closing the door behind her.

"When do you not have tea Rayna?" I said while laughing.

"Whatever. You have a new client coming in at 10. He came earlier but said he would return at his scheduled time. Chile, that man is fine! He was a little rough around the edges though." She said going on and on.

"I bet; if he needs my help. Get his file for me again so I familiarize myself with him before he comes." I said.

Every time one of my clients come in, Rayna tries to play match maker. She keeps saying I need to live a little. Quite frankly, she's right. Rayna has been my best friend for as long as I could remember. Her parents lived next door to us. Her dad was attorney as well. Although she's still in the field, she didn't want to be an attorney. Unlike my parents, her parents allowed her to be herself and live life. She's always been so free spirited. She lived a life I longed to live. I think that's why we clicked so well.

"Here you go!" She handed me his file.

Markell Davis, 25
Employed at Father's Mechanic shop.
Stopped for a routine traffic stop and drugs were found.

I sure hope it wasn't one of those cases where the defendant knew he was guilty. He has a pretty sticky past but seemed to have calmed down the last few years.

I read over his file some more and figured I knew a little bit about him. Let's see how it goes.

Chapter Two-Amira

"Hey Mira! Your 10am is here." Rayna said too excited for me.

"Okay, send him in."

"Good luck. He's a tough cookie to crack. "

I chuckled at her silly ass.

knock knock

"Come in!!" I yelled while I dated my notebook.

When I looked up I thought I seen a God himself. His mug shot definitely did him no justice. This man was fine. I don't know if it's because I haven't had sex in almost 2 years or if this man is just that fine; because a puddle was forming.

"You gon' continue to fuck me with your eyes or you going to introduce yourself?" He said bluntly.

I cleared my throat knocking out my trance. "Uh, excuse me?"

He chuckled showing his beautiful white smile. *God this man is fine.*

"Names Markell Davis."

"Amira -"

He cut me off. "Wright. The lawyer of the decade. I know."

"Very well then. Have a seat Mr. Davis. "

"Okay, I read over your case. This is some sticky stuff. Now, based on your past, this is a messy situation." I said.

"I get that, but I'm not my past. I made some dumb ass choices but I'm not a kid anymore. I'm a grown man trying to provide for my daughter." He said.

"You have a daughter? Is her mother around? "I asked.

He chuckled. "Is that your way of asking me if I'm with her mom?"

It was actually. "N- No. I just have to know what there is to know about my clients."

"I do and nah, I have custody of her. Her mom didn't want her because I loved her more."

"Oh wow. Sorry." I said. That was so selfish and stupid though.

"Nah, it's cool. Marlie is my world. She was my biggest blessing"

I admired his love for his daughter.

"Do you have enemies? Who would want to set you up like this?"

"My baby momma's people not fond of me. I don't know. I just know it wasn't mine. I went to the bar after work for one beer. And was headed home."

"Well I'm going to work on getting the footage from the bar. I'm also going to visit your job. I will need statements of your work hours. Okay?" I said.

"That's it?" He asked.

"Yes. They will inform me of trial date, and we can meet again on Thursday." I said while getting out myself to walk him out.

"Um, I know it may be inappropriate, but can I take you out? Lunch?" He asked.

"I'm afraid that is a bit of conflict of interest Mr. Davis." I said.

He chuckled cockily and walked close as hell to me; bend down to my ear and whispered, "Guess I'll see you Thursday. I'll bring lunch." Then nibbled on my ear and walked out.

I released the breath I was holding in. *Goddamn he was fine.*

CHAPTER 3 -Amira

I couldn't believe how bothered I was by this man. My thoughts were short lived when Rayna barged in.

"That fine ass man left smirking. What happened?" She asked.

"Nothing. We meet again on Thursday." I said nonchalantly

"Uhhhmmm, sure. You need some dick in your stuck-up ass anyways." She said laughing.

"Shut up! Go do some work man!" I said jokingly.

I had to get my mind right and focus on the matter at hand. I truly believe he's innocent. I'll do what I can to prove it. I must try to get all the evidence I'll need for this case to succeed. I finished my outline for this case, and I think I have the direction I want to go with. Seems as though all my colleagues turned down this case because it's too "messy". I can handle it.

Sunday and Mondays my parents have dinner at their home. The most dreadful days of the week for me. After work, I normally head over to their place.

"Rayna, I'm headed out babe." I said while headed out.

"Same here. Still headed to your parents huh?" She asked while laughing.

"Don't remind me. Sunday is enough." I said

"I don't know why you go on Mondays too. You act like its mandatory." she said

"I know, but you know how they are."

"Yes, I do, which is more than enough reason NOT to go." She said.

"Well with this case, this may be my last Monday for a minute." I said as we locked up and spoke to security.

"Oh, now this I got to see. Call me later. You're not off the hook yet. "

"Later girl!"

My Parent's House

"Ma, dad!" I yelled as I greeted Norma.

Norma is this older woman who practically raised us. My parents are so extra; however, I thank God for Norma. Norma not only made sure we were fed and bathe, but she gave the motherly affection that we lacked. My mom wasn't a bad mom, her world just revolved around my dad, her reputation and the firm. She left no time for her kids.

"Hey No-no!" I kissed her cheek.

"Hey baby. I cooked your favorite. Your snotty parents are waiting for you with your sisters and their husbands." She said laughing.

"Oh lord, help me. Okay."

"Hey guys." I said while walking into the room.

"Oh, hey darling. Glad you made it!" My mom said as I hugged everyone.

"We have a special guest coming."

"You look cute sis." my sister Aliyah said.

"Thanks, you too."

"How was your day?" Daddy asked.

"Good. Started on a new case today." I said as No-No poured me some water.

"Which one?" He asked.
"The Davis case." I said.

He was about to speak until the doorbell rung signaling this guest was here.

When I turn around, I swore my blood pressure rose through the roof. I even heard No-No cursing under her breath in Spanish. I knew my anger was evident.

"Hello Kyle, nice of you to join us!" my mom said excitedly.

He greeted everyone as he tried to kiss my cheek, but I immediately moved my head. He frowned then had a seat.

"Well Amira, that's no way to greet your guest." My mom said.

"He's your guest mom." I said nonchalantly. I was furious I started eating to avoid lashing out. *How dare they invite him here?*

"So, Amira, you took on the Davis case?" Daddy and Anya asked.

"Good luck with that." Kyle said. I ignored his comment and spoke up.

"Yes, I did. Everyone else denied it, but I'm taking on the challenge and plan to have succeed with it."

"How's that? He got caught with the drugs?" Kyle said again.

"Oh Amira, that's why it was denied. No way he's innocent." Aliyah said.

"And how do any of you know? We're you there?" I asked getting quite offended.

"No, but were you?" Mom asked.

"I wasn't but will prove my client's innocence. Next subject please." I said, over my case as the subject.

"Oh, Kyle Darling, you said you had an announcement? Mom asked.

"Oh, yes ma'am. Of course." He wiped his mouth and dug in his pocket.

He began getting on his knees and I couldn't believe this clown. I could see my family all smiles, but that was soon going to change. No-No walked out because she was bound to flip any minute.

"Amira Janae Wright, I know I made some mistakes and I regret them all; but I can't picture myself with anyone else. Will you marry me?"

I looked at him to see if he was crazy or not. "Are you kidding me? Am I being punked?" I said.

"Amira, you better say yes this minute!" My mom yelled.

"Hell no!" I yelled slamming my glass in the process.

"Alright Amira, you will respect your mother." My dad ordered.

"I can't believe you all. I'm out of here. Goodnight family!" I stormed out.

I heard my mother say, "Where did I go wrong with that one? Sorry Kyle. She'll come around."

Maybe in my next life.

I heard them calling my name, but I was over it. I can't believe they set me up like that.

Chapter 4-Amira

I finally made it home and headed to shower. In the midst of my shower my mind drifted to Markell. I have no clue why my mind was on him, but it was. I felt myself reaching for my treasure as I pictured him making love to me. I began rubbing lazy circles in my clit sending a sensation through my body.

"Ohh Markell" I began speeding it up as I pictured him thrusting in and out of me.

"Oh, my goddddddddddd"

"Oh, my goddddddddddd is right you nasty heffa"

"Rayna?" I said embarrassed.

"Yes, it's me. Hurry and get out I'm hungry."

I got out highly frustrated that I couldn't get my orgasm. However, I knew Rayna's impatient ass would give me hell.

"How the hell you get in Rayna?"

"Maybe with the spare you gave me."

"You should've called, I could have been having sex." I said.

"Yes sure. All I seen was you wishing you were sexing your client. Hell, I don't blame you. That man is fine." Rayna said.

"Whatever. I'm hungry too though."

"You didn't eat at your parent's?"

"Hell no! As a matter fact, I stormed out. You would never guess what they did."

I filled her in on what happened, getting upset all over again.

"Girl what? Okay, I don't know who's crazier, your parents or Kyle. I mean he really thought you were going to say yes. I can't deal." She laughed.

My phone started ringing knocking me out my thoughts. It was an unknown number.

"Amira Wright speaking."

He chuckled. "You even sound sexy over the phone ma."

"Markell?" Rayna was all ears then.

"Yes ma, it's me. Are you doing okay?"

"Yeah I'm fine. What do I owe the pleasure of this call? After work hours?"

"I know you said your cellphone is for emergencies. However, I think I know who may be a part of this. I couldn't wait until Thursday to tell you." He said sounding sexy.

I grabbed a pen and my notebook. "Okay talk to me."

"A lady came by the shop today saying she's been praying for me. She said she overheard it's my baby momma plotting on me to get my daughter back. She was pissed and so was her family..."

"So, they want to make you seem unfit."

"Exactly." He said.

"This is good Kell. I think it's pretty random though, but really good, nevertheless. We will add this on. We'll discuss more on Thursday."

"Kell? Oh, we on nickname basis now?"

"Whatever, it slipped."

"Sure, it did Mira. I'll see you on Thursday love."

With that we hung up and Rayna was eyeing me down smirking.

"What?" I asked.

"Girl you like him and it's all in your grill."

"Oh whatever. I do not. He's a nice guy though. It's strictly business." *It is, isn't it?*

Chapter 5-Markell

Something about Ms. Amira intrigues me. I don't know if it's her businesslike manner or if it's how beautiful she is. I could tell she doesn't wear much makeup, but she's still naturally beautiful. However, she's my lawyer so I must respect that. I only heard about how good of a lawyer she is, however I never met a lawyer that looked like that. When she looks at me, I see pain. I'm not sure of what she's been through. I vowed to never really get involved with another woman after that stunt Tiffany pulled. I don't even know why I care. It's something about her. She probably thinks I'm just some thug though.

I won't lie and say I don't have a past, but who doesn't? I'm just a real standup guy with dreams; that's all. I hope one day I can have my own everything. As much as I love working at my pop's shop, my passion is cooking. Just something I picked up. While locked up, I earned a culinary trade. My family taught me all the dos and don'ts of the kitchen growing up and it became a passion of mine. However, no one wants to hire an ex-Con. So one day, I'll own my very own restaurant or food business in addition to other things I've been working on. I'm just ready to provide a better life for my daughter. Hopefully I can get all this mess off my back.

"You know God will make a way of no way son." My mom said as she brought me out of my thoughts.

"I know momma, I know. I just hate that when I'm doing good, some stuff like this happens." I said.

"God allows certain things to happen in your life to make you a better you son. I'm proud of your change. He knows your heart. Let's hope this lawyer you speak so highly of can help prove that." she said as she kissed my forehead.

We live in a nice four-bedroom home that I helped my father build. I started building a home on my grandfather's land, but didn't have the money to complete it, as far as utilities and furniture goes. Unfortunately, I almost completed it before I got caught up with drugs. My parents said they would loan me the money to move in, but I depend on them enough. I don't want to live check to check and if I move now, that's exactly what it'll be. I've been saving up, but in due time. I'll keep the faith.

"Daddyyyyyy." Marlie yelled as she ran in. She just got back from school.

"Hey, Daddy's, big girl. How was your first day of Kindergarten?" I asked.

"Ooh, good daddy. I met new friends. My favorite friend is Kylie. Can Kylie play with me after school sometimes?"

"Well we will have to make sure it's okay with her parents. I'm sure it'll be okay!" I said.

"Oh goodie!! Sometimes her mommy can come and sometimes her nanny come she say. "

I chucked. "Okay baby girl. Go 'head inside. I have your pajamas out already. Grandma is waiting to give you a bath." I said.

"Where you going daddy? Can I go please?" She gave me those eyes I couldn't deny.

"Let me make sure it's okay." He said dialing Amira's number.

"Amira Wright speaking."

"Good afternoon Amira."

"Afternoon Mr. Davis. You aren't cancelling today's meeting are you?"

"No I'm not, but my daughter kind of wants to follow. She's very well behaved."

"Oh that's fine. I wouldn't mind meeting her as a matter of fact."

"Okay. I'm on my way."

"See you then."

I could tell she's blushing. "Let's head on out Marlie"

"Yahya! I'm going with daddy." Marlie sung while following me.

"Ma, Marlie coming with me."

"Got you again huh?" My mom asked while laughing.

"All the time." I said.

Chapter 6-Amira

I finally got the footage from the bar and opted on waiting on Markell to watch it. I was organizing papers when Rayna walked in.

"I see you're boo coming today." She said

"He's not my boo."

"Uhhmm. Marco's for drinks later?" She asked.

"Sure. You'll have me being the 3rd wheel again." I said.

"You're not a third wheel. You could even invite Markell. "She said

"Whatever. How was Kylie's first day of school?"

"Good. She blabbed on and on about her new best friend and how she wants to do play dates. I told her yeah and that I would talk to the girl's mom tomorrow; but forgot I have a doctor's appointment."

"I can pick her up and meet the parent for you." I said.

"Oh great, thanks babe. Looks like your man walking in." she said walking out.

"Hush and bring him in."

In walked Mr. Markell with a beautiful daughter in tow. I see Rayna looking confused, but I gave her that "I'll tell you later." look.

"Hello Mr. Markell and you must be Ms. Marlie." I said.

She giggled. "Yes ma'am. My name is Marlie Rae Davis. My daddy named me that." She said.

She's the cutest thing ever.

"Well nice to meet you. My name is Amira."

"I like your name and your hair is very pretty." She said

"Why thank you." I said.

"Amira, go watch your tablet on the sofa over there. Let daddy and Ms. Amira talk for a minute."

She pouted for a minute, but went to play her game.

"She's so sweet and very well mannered." I said.

"Ahh thanks. She's something else. Never a dull moment."

"I admire you. Not too many single dad's out there. Especially raising a daughter." I said.

"Thanks. Yeah, it's something. Thank God for my mom helping out from time to time. "

"Support systems are awesome." I said with a hint of sadness. I cleared my throat getting to the matter at hand. "So I have some footage. I haven't watched it yet because I wanted to wait for you." I said changing the sore subject.

"Okay, cool."

I couldn't help but notice how well behaved his daughter was.

"Marlie I have coloring books and colors as well. They are for someone your age. "

"Amira you don't have to. "He said.

"No, its fine. My god daughter comes a lot, so that's why they are here."

"Oh yes Ms. Amira." Marlie said excitedly. I handed her everything. "Thank you Ms. Amira."

"You are welcome baby."

"She's too precious Markell."

He chuckled showing that sexy grin. "Thanks ma. I tried to teach her the importance of little things and not all material things." He said.

I nodded

We started watching the footage and finally came to the area when he approached the bar. I timed it. He made it at 6:30 pm. The footage shows the inside and outside. We watched the footage very intently and that's when a black sedan pulled up right beside his vehicle around 7:30pm.

"Dammit, I didn't lock my doors."

"$1 in the swear jar daddy." Marlie said not looking up from her coloring.

He handed her a dollar and I chuckled at it.

I immediately got serious when I see someone get out the car. They had a black duffle bag and placed it in his car. The person looked around, got in the vehicle and sped off.

I looked over at Markell and his anger was evident. He was pissed, and quite frankly he has every right to be. I don't understand how he was even charged. I find it very fishy that this footage was not used as evidence.

"This some BS man!" He said.

"It is. Now I'm going try to get this plate cleared up and traced. This will be used in court. It's right there. Just make sure your story remains the same as it did when you were stopped. I'm visiting your job tomorrow and getting their statements for records. Do you think anyone would want to testify on your defense?" I asked.

"Anyone at the shop. They all know how and what I've been doing." He said.

"Great. I know you've got to get baby girl home, but I really need some more personal information to present in court." I said.

His trial was set for Monday and here we are on Thursday.

"Okay, I work until 4 tomorrow." he said.

I thought about what Rayna said. I didn't want to overstep my client and lawyer boundary, but our meeting before trial is tomorrow so I have to get this tonight.

"This may seem farfetched, but would you like to come Marco's? I normally go with my friend Rayna. She always leaves me for her boo. We can discuss over coffee or dinner or something?"

"Hmm sounds like a date ma!" He said smirking.

I blushed at his thoughts. "It is not!"

He chuckled. "Yeah I'll come ma." he said while getting up.

"Okay. Meet me there at 9?"

"I will be there. Come on Marlie, tell Ms. Amira bye." He said

"Bye Ms. Amira. Can I come see you again?"

"Sure babe. I'll bring my god daughter next time." I said.

"It was her eyes huh?" He asked.

"Yep. She's quite a charmer!"

"Works every time. See you later ma." He said as we winked and walked out.

Chapter 7-Amira

I was back home and out the shower trying to figure what to wear. We go to Marco's almost every week and here I am excited like I don't know what. I finally decided on a simple little outfit. I applied mascara, eyeliner and went on my way. I texted Rayna and Markell saying I was on my way. I didn't tell Rayna he was coming yet, she would've gotten overly excited.

Marco's

I walked in and rolled my eyes at the thirsty looks from the men and finally noticed Rayna at the bar munching on chips and queso.

"You save enough for me trick!" I joked.

"Girl this queso is the truth, but baby you are looking mighty fine."

Before I could respond I smelled Mr. Hand some's cologne.

"Hello Amira." his deep husky voice said.

"Oh, hey Markell. Glad you could make it. This is my assistant and best friend Rayna. I heard y'all met already." I said.

"We did. She was sassy." He joked

"Was not." she said playing innocent.

I saw her boo walking in.

"Well I see you're in good hands. Be back"

"Sure." I said.

"Could I offer you two anything?" the bartender asked.

"I just want Moscato and order of Marco's wings. What about you Kel?"

"Just get me a water and chips and queso."

"Coming right up!"

"I love their wings." I said.

"They are pretty good. I would add my special sauce to it though." He said.

"Special sauce? You're talking like you can cook or something." I said.

"I can actually. Got a degree while in prison in culinary. I plan to own something one day. Just been saving up and praying."

"Wow, impressive. Would have never guess that."

"There's a lot to learn about me. I applied places, but no one hires an ex-Con." he said

"Hey, it'll come. You never know when your blessing is looking you in the eyes." I said.

We stared at each other for a while before I cleared my throat and sipped my wine.

"Yeah, you're right." he said, obviously feeling the same way I felt.

We talked about a lot and he told me all his dreams and even about his home. It was quite amazing and I found myself more attracted to him by his ambition. He's been through a lot and he's a great father. We talked so much; I didn't realize it was about closing time. Rayna left an hour ago with her boo.

Just as we were about to get up Marco, the owner, came out.

"Hey Amira. Funny to see you still here. "

"Yeah, met up with a friend. Markell this Marco."

"Nice to meet you sir." Marco said.

"Pleasures all mine. I'm a huge fan of your work. "He said

"Ah. A chef?" He asked.

"Yes, got my license and degree."

"Where are you cooking son?"

Markell chuckled. "Besides momma's kitchen and family functions, nowhere due to my past record." He said.

Marco sat there for a while.

"His food is amazing." I lied. I haven't tasted any of his food. Markell was looking at me but I didn't look back.

"Is that so? Well Mr. Markell. Amira is picky on who she associates with, so I know you're good people. I trust her and she's like a daughter to me. I'm in need of a head chef. Come by on Saturday, show me what you got. If you're amazing like she's said, you got the job. Pay is good and if you enjoy cooking, it will not even feel like work."

"Thanks. Thanks so much. I'll be here!" Markell said.

"See you then." He kissed my forehead and left.

I smiled at this. I was so happy for him. This would be amazing for his case.

"What just happened here?" he asked in disbelief as we walked towards my car. "Thanks for inviting me ma. Thanks for vouching for me as well."

"No problem. Don't let me down. Now you have to really cook for me." I said.

"I will definitely do that."

"I have faith in this case and you. It'll be fine, don't worry. I had a nice night."

"I did too ma. I really did."

He looked at me and I wanted him to kiss me. He bent down and did just that. He kissed my lips softly asking for tongue access and I let him. We kissed passionately like we were a couple. He stopped and kissed my forehead.

"Let me know when you make it home beautiful." With that he walked away.

Oh my lord.

Chapter 8-Markell

Next Day

Mr. Marco wanted me to come in today instead and I was all for it. I told my dad and he was okay with me leaving early from the shop, especially when it involved something I'm passionate about. I went and got clean at home and made sure I had all the necessary paperwork with me. Marco told me to dress comfortably. I decided on some black jeans and a Red polo t-shirt. I noticed he and his employees wear red and black. If I want the job, why not look the part right?

This was the perfect thing to get my mind off how the meeting went with Amira. I pray things work in my favor, I really do. I'm not trying to leave Marlie behind something I didn't do. I worked hard to get custody of her. I know CPS are lurked out behind this case, one of the major reasons I'm praying to get through this.

I finally made it to Marco's. I took a deep breath and said a little prayer before walking in.

"Hey, I'm here to see Marco!" I told the young Mexican woman in the front.

"Oh, sí que está esperando para usted" (Oh, yes he's waiting for you.) she said.

"Huh?" I said

"Oh I'm sorry, sometimes I forget. I said he's waiting for you dear. I'm his wife Marcella, follow me."

I nodded and followed her. It was pretty quiet in here at this time.

"Marco, he's here!" She said while walking out.

"Ahh, hello Markell!! Glad you could make it. I see you dressed in the colors huh? Well if you get this, you will be rocking a fancy chef outfit like me." He said, boosting my confidence.

"That's right!" I said.

"Okay, So What do you want to do? Do you want to cook some menu items or something of your own?"

"How about I do both. I'll cook a few of your most popular items, plus one of my own in under two hours!"

"What?" Marco asked as If he was confused.

I pulled out a chair. "Yes, have a seat and watch me work Mr. Marco!" *Watch how I get to work in this here kitchen!*

Chapter 9-Amira

Sitting waiting for the other side to attend this meeting, I arrived early as always. I have a reputation and I will keep it up. The way the lawyer represents themselves reflects against the client. The judge walked in.

"Well Good morning Ms. Wright. I didn't know you were the counsel on this case." Judge McCain said.

"Yes sir! I'm representing the defendant Markell Davis." I said,

"Okay. Thanks for being punctual."

"No problem sir."

The other counsel walked in and we were ready to begin our meeting. I was a bit nervous, but I never seemed to let it show. I've handled bigger cases than this one before.

"Hello Judge McCain. Ms. Wright"

"Hello Mr. Rogers"

"Mr. Rogers." I smiled.

"Let's get this started. I know I said that the defendant wasn't necessary for attendance, but may I ask of his whereabouts for current records."

I remembered he text me this morning saying he was starting at Marco's today. I was about to exaggerate a bit, only because I knew he would get it.

"Yes, my client is currently at work."

"He works at a chop shop right?" Mr. Rogers asked being petty of course.

"Actually, He's currently at the upscale restaurant Marco's where he's going to be the new leading chef. He was getting paid to work at his dad's MECHANIC shop, but got offered this positon due to his skill and licenses."

The way the judge nodded I could tell he was impressed aside from Rogers.

"Okay. Now Rogers what is your argument?"

"Well the defendant was stopped for no signal light and upon stopping, his vehicle was searched where the drugs were found. Here is his previous record."

I rolled my eyes at him

"I see. What made them search the car? Something doesn't add up as to the reasoning behind the search. People have bags and purses in their back seat all the time. Will all people get searched? This could back fire so badly. However, this is something he was involved with before. Now, Ms. Wright. What is your argument?"

"Before I show this footage. I felt my client was not in obligation to be searched. Not making any accusations, but someone must've reported him to initiate this search which leads me to believe my client was set up. Not only that, there was no proper search warrant or any indication for a search was needed. However, you don't have to take my word alone. This footage is from the bar."

I could see Rogers get upset and worried. You see Rogers and I are always at each other's neck. My dad tried to set me up with him once and I refused him big time and he's been salty ever since. He always tries to beat me in a case.

I started the video and watched as he grew uncomfortable.

"We're you aware of this video Rogers?" The judge asked.

"No sir. I wasn't."

"We do not have enough evidence to charge this man. I'm dropping charges immediately. Case dismissed." The judge said

"But what about the person who did it??"

"I'm going to prove who is involved throughout this whole thing." I said.

"Again, meeting adjourned. No trial is needed. Case dismissed. Good day now." with that the judge left.

I smirked at Rogers.

"You think you are something special huh? Your lonely ass won't find the person."

"I'm far from lonely. I just don't want your tired ass. I will find out who it is you're covering." I chuckled and left him with the dumb look on his face.

He isn't slick by a long shot.

Guess I'll head over to Marco's and spread the good news.

Chapter 10-Markell

"This is impressive. Markell you are heaven sent. Not only is presentation amazing, it all tastes great. Your timing was amazing as well!" Marco said.

"Thank you, sir, Appreciate it!"

"You got the job! Head chefs here get 22.50 an hour with opportunity of raises. Okay with you? There's more where that comes from."

"That's more than okay with me. That's great! Thank you. This means the world to me. Especially with all that's going on. You're a blessing."

"So are you kid." He smiled at and gave me a manly hug.

"Honey, Amira's here to see Markell." his wife said.

"Go head on! See you on Monday chef."

I walked out and long behold beautiful herself. She was looking so scrumptious in that pencil skirt.

"Hey pretty lady." I said. She blushed.

"Hey Kel. Congrats. Heard you got it."

"I did. I owe you one. Thanks." I was happy until I realized she didn't mention the meeting. "What about the meeting Amira?"

"WELL..."

"Lay it on me." I just knew this shit was going to trial.

"Case dismissed!" She smiled.

"What! Seriously?"

She chuckled. "Yes, you're good. I still will find out who did this to avoid future issues. However, you're good."

We looked at each other until I knew I had to make a move. I kissed her passionately.

"Thank you baby girl" I said.

"No biggie." She blushed obviously flustered by the kiss.

"Have dinner with me." I said.

"When?"

"Tonight."

"On one condition. You cook at my place. 6 pm., don't be late." She said seductively and walked away leaving me there like I left her the other night. *This girl will be the death of me.*

I went home and showered. I told everyone the good news. I couldn't wait to get established. I decided on cooking something quick and nice for her. I got all my stuff and headed to the address she text me.

I made it to her spot in like 15 minutes. I must say, ma got a nice spot. I rang the doorbell.

"Hey, come in." She had sweats on and hair tired up in a messy bun. She looked flawless.

"Damn."

"That ugly huh?" She asked.

"Nah ma. You're beautiful. Don't anyone tell you that?" I asked

"No. Not really."

"Well I'm a real dude and I'm gone give you the real." She smiled and showed me the kitchen.

I began cooking right away. I decided on my special steak fajitas for tonight with my homemade banana pudding. She sat there watching me and I could tell she was feeling me. I won't lie and say I wasn't feeling her too.

Chapter 11-Amira

"What you thinking about ma?" he asked me.

"Honestly you."

He cut off everything and fixed him and me a plate. It smelled great. It was amazing. We both prayed silently and began digging in. I moaned as I ate.

"That good huh?" He asked.

"Awesome. This is amazing."

"You're amazing." He said causing me to blush. "Look Amira. I know what this is. However, you got your boy open. I want you."

I took a big gulp of my wine and took a deep breath.

"I want you too, it's just my parents and we just met, you were my client..."

"Amira, you're twenty-four. Time to live your life for you." He said while walking up to me and taking me out the chair.

I began to breathe unevenly just from this man this close to me.

"So quit playing me and let's try this. We are young and only live once."

"One day at a time?" I asked.

"Whatever you want ma."

We stared at each other for a minute and then he kissed me. We made out for a while and I was on fire.

He lifted me up and said, "Where's your bedroom?"

"Upstairs, last door on the left."

He carried me effortlessly, never breaking the kiss. He kicked the door open and placed me gently on the bed.

"Whenever you want me to stop, say so. We both grown and ain't no sense on fighting faith."

With that he removed my bottoms. I didn't have on under wear. He smirked and licked his lips. He began massaging my clit.

"Ohhh."

"Mm. You so wet ma"

Before I could say anything he began sucking hard on my clit, sending waves of pleasure my way. I've never been eaten out before and this was driving me crazy. He began sticking his tongue in and out and slowly entered a finger. My body was in over drive and my peak was near.

"Go ahead and cum for me Amira.", and with those words, I erupted all in his mouth and he slurped every drop. He got up and went clean himself up.

"As bad as I want to give you this dick, you deserved to be made love to. You not ready yet but baby when you are, I'll give it to you right. So we clear, that's my pussy." he said.

"Can you stay the night?" I asked completely flustered.

"Yeah. I'll stay." He smirked. *I can get used to this.*

Chapter 12-Amira

I woke up and noticed Markell wasn't in bed. I frowned. "Did he leave and not tell me?" I said to myself.

I went to bathroom to take care of hygiene. As I was walking down stairs, I started smelling food cooking and immediately started smiling.
I guess he didn't leave.

"Morning Kell." I said.

"Good morning beautiful. I cooked you a nice southern style omelet." He said as he kissed my forehead and placed a plate in front of me.

I took a bite right away and moaned at how good it was.

"This is amazing." I said.

"Glad you like it love." He said.

"So what do you have planned today?" I asked.

"Well, if you are free I wanted to take you to the house and show you what I'm working on; and then I have to pick up Marlie from school." he said.

"Sure. I don't mind at all. I don't have to go into the office today. What school your daughter goes to?" I asked while finishing up my food.

"Louisiana Academy." He said.

"Oh, that's where my god child goes. I'm picking her up today as well. "I said.

"Well you can just come with me pick up Marlie and we can kill two birds with one stone." he said.

"Sounds good. Let me wash these dishes and go get ready." I said.

"Nah you good ma! Go ahead and take care of your business. I will take care of the kitchen, go get dressed then I'll come back and scoop you up. Cool?"

"Yeah, that's fine." He kissed me softly as I walked upstairs.

I couldn't help but smile at his antics. He's amazing without even trying. Knowing my parents, they will try to destroy my happiness in a heartbeat. I will just cross that bridge when it gets there.

I decided to get ready for my day. I decided on my gray sweater and leggings and I'll wear my hair straight. I'm not applying any makeup, just going to be all natural today. I love chill days. Normally I'll have my hair in a messy bun, but I opted out of it today. I was pulled out of my thoughts by my phone ringing. Rayna was calling.

"Morning Ray Ray!" I said.

"Ray Ray? Uh uh, bitch spill it!"
I chuckled at her.

"Spill what?" I said.

"The reason you're so damn bubbly at ten am on your day off."

"If you must know, Kell and I had dinner and he stayed over and I woke up to breakfast." I said while blushing

"Amira! Did you finally get you know what?"
"Rayna really? No! However, he gave me some amazing head." I said.

"You mean to tell me that man cooked you dinner, stayed over, cooked breakfast and he didn't get any?"

"Yep!" I said popping the P.

"Oh baby, he's a keeper."

"We are just friends Rayna." I said trying to convince myself more than anything.

"Friends don't make you cum." She said laughing.

"Whatever! Did you still need me to pick up baby girl?" I asked

"If you can."

"Yes, I told Kell I would go with him pick up his daughter. Maybe they could get acquainted. "I said

"Oh yes, you like him to want to bring your godchild in it. You got Kylie spoiled rotten Amira!" Rayna said.

"That's Tee Tee's baby!" I said.

"Yea okay. Well I'm headed to the office a while before my doctor's appointment. Call or text me if you need. Love ya!"

"Love you too babe!"

Chapter 13-Amira

As I finished getting ready for the day, the door bell rung. I got all excited thinking it was Markell.

"Now you know…." My happiness was short lived when I realized it was my sister standing there.

"What do you want Anya?" I said.

"Well is that any way to greet your big sister? Where are you off to? It's ladies day with your sisters and mother." She said trying to let herself in.

"Well today is a bad day. I have plans!" I closed and locked the door.

"This is a weekly thing Amira. Mother will be upset!"

"Well it ends this week! I'm not going."

On cue Markell pulled up jamming pretty Ricky loud. I snickered at the look on my sister's face. She looked totally taken back by not only a guy pulling up, but a guy like Markell. This was a sight to see.

Markell got out and said

"You ready baby?" While kissing my forehead. My sister looked with her mouth dropped. I knew Markell was about to be in petty mode. This was hilarious.

"Oh pardon me, I'm Markell and you are?"

"I'm her sister, what are you doing here? Aren't you her client?" She asked appalled.

"None of your business Anya. I'm not going to be attending the festivities today." I said as we walked to the car and pulled off.

"Wait until mom and dad hears how you are rebelling." She yelled.

"That felt so good!" I said to Kell.

He chuckled. "Baby girl that means you have to free yourself more often. Your family can't control you."

I nodded in understanding because he was right.

We drove for another 20 minutes until we landed in a beautiful area, one I never knew existed. We finally pulled up to a beautiful two story home. It was amazing.

"This is it." He said as he helped me out the car.

"This is beautiful. You built this?" I asked in amazement.

"Yes, with the help of my dad and a few of his friends. This is all my ideas. I invested some of the bad money into supplies, but the rest is hard earned saved money. Due to Marlie's schooling and all her needs money wise, I was unable to finish things off."

We walked inside and was breathtaking.

"Finish what off?"

"The utilities aren't on yet and furniture and stuff. Thankfully, I got this job at Marco's with weekly pay and I can slowly start getting this together. I know my mom loves me there, but I'm done being a burden."

"Wow, this is awesome. Awfully big house for you two." I said.

"Hmm. Maybe one day it won't be just us two, if you catch my drift." He said. I blushed.

We sat on deck just talking about everything. I learned more about his past as he did mines. He couldn't believe I allowed my parents to treat me as they did. My parents were calling me nonstop. My dad left me a message saying he was going to have my house foreclosed if what Anya said was true. She went and told them all these things that quick. She doesn't know what's going on.

"Seriously though Amira, why do you let them? You are not a kid anymore." He said.

"Well for starters, I work for their firm. They paid my way through school. "

"Amira, you are the best lawyer there. You can start you own firm. I'm sure whoever works under you will follow. They may have paid your tuition, but YOU did the work. You earned your degree, passed the bar and license to practice. They didn't pay for that. Your hard work and dedication did."

"Where will I live?"

"Is that a trick question?"

"Markell, don't even think about it!"

"Amira, you can start over. Women do it every day. You need to stop being afraid of change. Although it's different, different isn't always scary."

"It isn't always better either."

"How would you know though?" He said.

"I guess you are right."

"I know I am woman! Don't worry about them right now. Let's go get these girls!" He said.

Chapter 14-Amira

We made it to the school and the girls were walking out holding hands laughing.

"I guess they know each other." I said.

"Hey daddy!! Hey Ms. Amira!" Marlie said.

"Hey, you know my nanny?" Kylie asked.

"Yes, she's my daddy's friend. Daddy this my friend."

"Oh, this is the friend you both were talking about!!"

"Small world huh?"

"Very!"

The girls were so excited to leave with each other. I text Rayna a picture of them and explained everything. She said they could have a sleepover being that it's Friday night. They were thrilled. It was too cute. We went over to Markell's mom and dad's house to get Marlie's belongings.

We arrived to a nice home with a very beautiful yard. I see that this family takes pride in their homes. Very beautifully built. Not two story, but beautiful nevertheless.

We walked in and he screamed, "Ma, I'm here!"

"Boy, stop hollering in my house." She said while walking towards us. "Oh, hello there. Who might you be?" She asked.

"This is Amira ma."

"Oh you are the infamous Amira that has his nose wide open like that. I'm Evelyn, but you can call me Mama E or Mama or MAAAAA, like your boy here screams"

"Maaaa." He said embarrassed. It was cute.

"Oh hush. Is this your daughter?" She asked.

"No, this is my godchild who happens to be friends with Marlie. Nice to meet you." I said.

"Pleasure's all mine."

"Ma, Marlie is going to a sleepover. We came to get her things before dropping her off. I'm going to get that. Try not to scare Amira away." He said while walking off.

"He's something else. Follow me dear, let me introduce you to my husband."

"Honey, this is Amira."

"Oh, hi there darling. Heard a lot about you. Appreciate what you did for my boy! He's really a changed man. He told me about the chef job too. All he does is blab about you. He said you were beautiful, but that's an understatement."

"Aww thanks!"

"He's always flirting." Ms. Evelyn said.

"Oh, ain't nobody flirting. Just making my future daughter in law feel loved." He said while walking out laughing.

I started laughing. "He's too much. I see where Kell gets it from."

"Honey, you don't know the half of it!"

We talked for a while and I promised to visit again.

We finally were headed to drop the girls off at Rayna's. I decided to get out and drop them.

"Ready to go?" He asked.

"Yes sir!"

We pulled up to my house and as we got down my heart dropped.

"You got to be fucking kidding me!"

A "**For Sale** "Sign was in the yard. They managed to do this that fast.

"Man, your people are ridiculous." He said. We walked in and things were all over. They came in and dug everywhere. What type of shit is this?

"You might want to read this." Kel said handing me a note.

"Either you hang up this phase with this hoodlum or you have 24 hours to be out.
Dad"

They owned this house and are capable. They've done this with my sister but of course she gave in. I started crying out of frustration.

"No baby girl. You will NOT let them break you. That's what they want. Get all the things you need and own now. I'll help you. I'm not taking no for an answer Amira. Put shit in boxes, we'll call up my boys to bring the shit to my new house. They will take as much as they can tonight. Things will be okay. Get what you need for tonight and tomorrow morning and we can stay at a hotel tonight, I'll stay with you."

"Markell..."

"No Amira. It's done!"

Chapter 15-Markell

In no time my cousins were here moving things in a huge moving truck. She was able to get her bed room set and stuff in there as well. It took a total of 3 hours and we took basically everything she needed including TVs. It was about midnight and they were bringing everything over. I couldn't believe all that was happening to her so quickly.

We made it to the Hilton downtown and checked in for the rest of the week. I know she will need it to get things in order. While she's doing that, I'll get things in order on my end as well.

Amira hasn't said a word since we made it here. I know it's all hitting her at once, but enough is enough with that shit. She helped me, now I'm going help her.

I heard loud cries and I knew she was breaking down.

"Calm down baby...breathe!"

"Why me? This has been going on all my life and I've had enough!" She said through tears.

"I got you. Let me take care of you. Can I do that?" She nodded.

I picked her up gently and carried her to one of the beds. I lay her down and admired her beautiful body. I kissed her and whispered, "You are so beautiful baby."

I move my hand down her silky skin as she began to kiss me harder and moan. I began kissing her neck and collarbone gently. I softly bite her ear lobe, making her moan louder and faster. She released her grip on my shoulders, and unbuttons my shorts. Her hands were in sync with our lips, as she reaches underneath my boxers. It's my turn to release a moan.

She whispered, "Do you like it?"

In between our kisses I whispered back, "Yes, but not yet.", pull her hands out of my boxers and above her head. I wanted to make love to her and please her.

I move my lips lower and lower, reaching her breasts. I glanced at her, taking in her beauty. She willfully keeps her hands above her head, giving me permission to explore her further. I continue kissing lower and lower, resting my hands on her breasts. She moans more frequently, cheering me to go all the way. She sits up and kisses me, breaking to pull my shirt off.

"I want you." she says, putting her arms over my head. "Never before have had I felt such a connection."

"You got me." I said.

After a minute of playful teasing, her hands find themselves pulling down my shorts. I smile and pin her down on the bed. "Not until I get my turn." I say. I kiss my way down until I'm at the spot that drives her wild. Every twist and jerk of her body makes me lick faster. Eventually she pulls my head up, telling me she's ready. Our lips never part the whole time I'm inside her. Each thrust forces her breathing to speed up. Each thrust in tune with her rhythmic motion. She puts my hand over her mouth, embarrassed of her moaning. "Let that shit out Amira".

I nibble on her ear and speed up, hoping to make her orgasm. I slow down at points so I don't orgasm before her. After twenty minutes, she arches her back and exhales slowly. I stop to watch her act it out before she grabs my neck violently and says, "Keep going."

After ten more minutes I could not hold myself anymore and I came even with her.

I rolled over and caught my breathe. My mind was racing with a million words to describe how I feel about Amira. Feeling increasingly tired, we roll over and cuddle until we both were sound asleep. Every corner of my mind completely weightless. It was a serenity I have never felt. This girl was bringing out another side to me.

Chapter 16-Amira

I woke up sore, but it was a good sore. I just laid there for a moment replaying last night's events. So much has happened in so little time and I know today is going to be even more eventful.

"Morning beautiful." He said with a towel around his waist looking lovely.

"Morning handsome."

I got up and went take care of my hygiene.

"What does today have planned for you?" I asked him.

"Well, I'm going to the house to get some things in order and make sure your stuff's straight."

"About that Markell…"

He cut me off. "End of discussion on that ma. I'm not asking for you to marry a nigga. I don't even have to stay there with you if it makes you feel uncomfortable. You can't stay in this hotel until you find a spot."

There was no use in protesting because he was right. I don't know how my parents will react to me moving out, they are bound to get rid of me at the office and wasting money at a hotel would not be smart; no matter how much I have saved.

"I guess you are right."

"You know I am. I got to go by the restaurant for a while afterwards, then get Marlie. My mom went and get her this morning. What you got planned?"

"Well, unsure of how my parents going to react once they got the hint that I moved all my shit, I'm going gather up my things at the office then honestly, start building shopping I guess."

"Call me if you need me. Your car is already outside. My homeboy and I went and got it early this morning. I knew you were going to be busy today. Remember what I told you and come by for lunch okay?"

"Okay, I will." With that we kissed passionately. We stared at each other for a while.

"Look about last night..."

"We will talk about it later Amira. Just know I got you, okay?" I nodded. We shared another kiss and he walked out leaving me in my thoughts.

"Guess I'll start this day."

I braced myself as I walked into work. I didn't know what to expect. Dealing with my parents was a roller coaster. However, I was tired of being on their ride. Something has got to give.

"Good morning Ms. Wright." one of my male colleagues said.

"Morning!" I responded.

Despite my nervousness, I was in a good mood. I chuckled at the reasoning behind that. I didn't see Rayna at her desk. I wondered where she was. I made it to my office and she was in it waiting for me. I forgot I gave her spare key to that too.

"Morning Ray!"

"Morning girl. You have a message from your dad and baby I almost cursed him out, with his ugly ass attitude." She said.

"Girl. You don't know the half of it!"

"SPILL!"

I told her everything from the situation about my house, sleeping with Kell, his home, him wanting me to stay there. I basically spilled some freshly brewed tea.

"Baby, my cup runneth over with this tea!" We both burst out laughing. This girl is crazy man. "But it all seriousness, this is going too far. I say take a chance. I know it's risky, but when have you ever taken a risk. Everything you have ever done has been planned out thoroughly by your parents. You should do this; live a little. Hell, you can get that good D regularly now baby!" she said laughing.

"Rayna, we are not even together for me to move in with him."

"No doubt in my mind y'all are going to end up together. Besides, he simply stated he doesn't have to stay there. You can look at it as a living arrangement, sort of like roommates until you guys have a "title"; which nowadays, doesn't mean anything. I do get what you saying, but I still say go for it. Show your parents you are not what THEY say you are, but who you say you are." Rayna said. Quite frankly, she was absolutely right.

"Not only that, I know this job is the next thing on their petty list." I said.

"It may be, but your license can't be taken away nor can your degree. YOU are an attorney because YOU did the work. You have money saved up. We can start over."

"We?" I asked.

"Hell yeah! You think I'm going to stay here? I'm only here because of you. You know you parents agg me more than mine do."

"I wish I had your courage."

"You do. Use it. "

"You are right. Let's go to Marco's for lunch and look at this building I looked up. Then maybe I can start packing up this office just in case."

"Sounds good to me."

Chapter 17-Amira

I made sure everything was a go for the meeting. I had all the necessary paperwork and all. I made copies of everything for Rayna to keep and to give to the appropriate people at the meeting. All my valuables and important documents were packed up and ready to go. I made sure to keep originals in a safe deposit box. I brought some of it to my vehicle just in case my parents pulled some crazy shit, then we finally decided to head out to Marco's.

We finally made it and it wasn't as busy, which was good for me. I wanted to chill.

"Hello my beautiful ladies. How are you two?" Marcella asked.

"We're good. We'll take our regulars. Sangria's too!" I yelled.

"Long day huh?" Marco walked out and hugged us.

"You don't know the half of it." I sighed.

"Tell me about it. Markell should be returning soon. He went out and ran an errand for me."

"How is he doing here?"

"Great! He took care of lunch rush sooo quickly. He's so efficient, not to mention he can cook." Marco said.

We talked for a while and I told him everything. He knew some of it. I assumed Kel told him, which is fine. He was extremely upset. He wanted to go see my dad, but I stopped him.

On cue, Markell walked in. "Hey Rayna, hey babe." He hugged her and kissed me.

"Well alright Nah." Rayna said.

"Can I talk to you for a minute ma?" Kel asked.

We excused ourselves from the conversation with Marco and Rayna.

"What's up love?" I asked.

"I know you are independent and all for doing things yourself. However, I wanted to give it a push. I found you a building. My aunt is a real estate agent and just so happens a loyal customer here. She came in earlier and mentioned this business. I told her I knew of someone who may or may not be interested." He said.

I didn't say anything for moment. "Wow really. Where is it? How much is it because I have to be careful with my decisions."

He showed me the picture and ironically it's the building I was eyeing.

"This is the same building Rayna and I were going to look at!" He smiled and called them over.

"Yep and it's yours!" I said.

"Wait what? How? Markell this had to be expensive."

"Let's say my aunt loves her nephew. It wasn't expensive. "

"And Marco and I paid that." Marcella said.

"What? Why?"

"You are like a daughter to us. You have brought business to us. When business was bad, you were faithful to us and donated. Now we are one of the wealthiest restaurants in Louisiana. We watched you go through school and become this successful lawyer. It's our thank you and gift to you."

I was at lost for words.

"I don't know what to say. I haven't even been fired yet."

"That's fine. That gives us time to get the place ready legally and make it look good. U can put the stuff you don't need on hand at that spot. Take it one day at a time; then if and when they do it, you'll be prepared." Rayna said.

Everything was so overwhelming. "Thanks so much you guys."

We headed back to the office for a while. I finished everything and got my things to head over to the hotel.

"Ready to roll Rayna?" I asked.

"Yes ma'am. Kylie is going to her dad for a couple of days and I'm already missing her. "

"Oh really. I'm glad y'all on speaking terms again."

"Girl yeah. He's in town at his mom's for the week, so I'll let her go. He went to get her from school and she was so excited she made him call me."

"Aww she loves her daddy. She does. "

Chapter 18-Amira

We hugged and parted ways until tomorrow. We were going to check on the building. I'm debating on going to church. I'm only debating because I have to face my parents. However, it's time to do it.

I made it back to the hotel and showered until Markel and Marlie got there. I was going to tell him I accepted his offer on moving in. I also wanted to talk to him about where we stood with one another.

I was yanked out my thoughts when I heard a knock on the door. It was Markel and Marlie.

"Hey guys."

"Hey Ms. Mira. I drew you a picture. "
I chuckled at her eagerness to see me.

"Wow, this is so pretty." I said.

"Yayyy!"

I gave him the look signaling I wanted to talk. I put it on the cartoons for her.

"Watch cartoons while daddy talks to Ms. Mira."

"Ok daddy."

We stepped to the side a bit to talk.

"What's wrong bae? "He asked

"I decided that I'll move in, however I need to know where we stand. Like what are we?" I asked

"We can be whatever you want. I told you that. You're mine Amira." I blushed at him and pecked his lips.

"You're mine too Kel."

We made it to the house and Marlie was in her own world, not realizing what was going on. Obviously I was oblivious to the fact as well, because when I walked in I was in awe. Everything was decked out and beautiful.

"Take a look."

We looked everywhere and everything was beautiful. "How did you manage to get all of this done?"

"I have my ways." He smirked.

We stopped at a door with an M on it.

"Marlie. I have a surprise for you."

"Ooohh...What is it daddy?" He opened the door and Marlie and I both gasped.

"Oh, my godddddddddddd. Daddy it's filled with princesses. I want a room like this!"

"Baby, this is your room." He said.

She started squealing a jumping and playing with all the toys. It was the cutest scene ever.

"You're the best daddy in the world." She said.

This was so cute. Bittersweet, I wished I had the bond they shared with my dad.

"Time for bed kiddo."

She pouted for a while but she was sleepy. After he finally got her in, I took this time to thank him. I kissed him passionately.

"Thanks so much. This is all so much" He led me to the room and my jaw dropped at how beautiful everything was. "Babe."

He cut me off by kissing me deeply

"Let's make love on our new bed. This all may be sudden, but fate has no time frame."

He removed my shorts and panties in one swift motion, then began feasting on my pearl right away.

"Oohhh..."

"Feels good bae?" He asked as he started fingering my G-spot.

"Yesssss"

He got up and started stroking his manhood, only making me wetter. He pulled out a condom and entered me right away.

"Fuck!" we said in unison as he entered me slowly.

He began thrusting in and out slowly driving us both crazy. The sounds of our lovemaking were all that was heard. We kept it down not wanting to wake up Marlie.

"Mm. Right there Kel..."

He began pounding my spot over and over. I felt myself tighten around him and I knew my orgasm was near. We went on until we both released.

"Kel..?"

"Shh...I love you too.

Chapter 19-Amira

Sunday Morning

  I woke up right before my alarm was set to go off. It was about 8 am. Church began at 11 today. I decided to get up and cook breakfast. Rayna insisted I invited Kell and Marlie. I was skeptical at first, but I need to step up and do it. I'm doing it. I made French toast with eggs and bacon.

  "Morning beautiful." He said while walking in the kitchen kissing my forehead.

  "Morning hun. I made a small breakfast. It's not like yours, but my toast is to die for." I said while laughing.

  On cue, Marlie came and we ate. I offered to get Marlie ready for church. This was going to be an eventful day and I'm ready for it.

  We made it to church the same time as Rayna. "This is my parent's church!" He said.

  "Really? I don't know how we never noticed each other."

  "Yeah, that's their car over there." He said.

  Marlie went along with Rayna into church while Markell and I sat in for a minute since we were early.

  "Are you sure you want to do this?" He asked.

  'Yes, didn't you say I needed to stand up for myself?"

  "Yes I did and you do, but for you. Not for me." He said.

"I want to do this; I need to do this." He nodded, kissed my forehead and we got out.

Rayna waited for us by the door. "About time. Thought y'all was trying to get freaky on the lord's grounds." She said laughing.

"Let's go girl!"

We finally walked in and greeted everyone. We hugged his parents and sat down. My parents and sisters were not here yet, but I'm sure it won't be long. My heart was beating so fast.

"It'll be fine. Don't fret them." Rayna said.

Marlie and Kylie sat quietly coloring. They are so well behaved.

My parents walked in. I figured they knew I was here because we came in my car. They all have been on reject list since the house situation. I didn't want to have any conversations with them. I took them off reject this morning. I noticed my mom scanning the church for me and when she finally noticed me she had this mean glare. They sat upfront. My mom noticed me, but no one else did. I was expecting an outburst, but I guess she contained herself since we were in church.

Church was amazing. I felt like the message was speaking directly to me. The pastor's message was centered on 2 Corinthians 5:7 which is one of my favorite bible scriptures. "Walk by faith and not by sight." That was all the confirmation I needed. After that, I'm ready to live my life for me. Rayna and I were waiting outside of church talking with Kel's parents. Kel was still speaking with pastor. "Well hello daughter." my mother came and spoke with my sisters in tow.

"Hello mother, sisters." I said dryly.

"We've been trying to reach you all week."

"I know. I've had you all on reject list." I said bluntly.

They look taken back by my response and I didn't care.

"Excuse me? Little girl..." My dad came cutting her off.

"Well hello daughter. I take it you got my message and you will end this thing you have going on." he said in matter factually tone.

I chuckled. "I did get your messages and I will not be ending anything but this discussion with you all." Before my dad could get a sassy remark in, Markell came in.

"Sorry I took a while babe, you ready?" He asked as he kissed my forehead.

I noticed my dad clench his jaw and my mom get upset. I also noticed the envy in my sister's eye.

"Oh my apologies, I'm Markel-" My mom cut him off.

"We know who you are and what you are about!" She spat.

His mom was about to say something, but he stopped her.

"All due respect ma'am, but you don't know a thing about me. You may have heard some things, but you don't know me."

"Sir, we know enough to know you are to leave my daughter alone because you will not have a penny of my money. Matter of fact, Amira the house is sold and you may want to reconsider this thing because your job is at stake as well." My dad said.

I could see Markell clenching his jaw and his parents trying to keep their composure on church grounds.

"Now you've said enough! You will not talk to my son like that!" His dad said coming into my dad's face.

"I don't want a penny of your money. I make my own the right way. Establishing myself in my career without a handout." He said.

"And I make my own decisions now! I'm sick of you two trying to run my life. My sisters may choose to be married and live the life you want, but I will not go on like this! Do what you have to do!" I said while grabbing Kel's hand and turning on my heel.

My dad chuckled. "You work for me daughter!"

"Not anymore. Consider yourself one attorney short, the best one at that. Let's see how successful your firm remains without me."
Rayna began following me to our car.

"Oh and Ms. Rayna, you still work for me. If you entertain this parade, you can consider yourself fired along with her."

"I quit as well. I'm rolling with my best friend."

I loved the look of shock on my moms and sister's face. My dad tried to remain unfazed, but he was appalled as well and I didn't give a damn. I'm sick of these people. My life starts now!

"You will be nothing without me! You are dead to me if you rebel! I will disown you! Thrown to wolves!" He yelled.

I heard my mom saying that it was enough, but the damage was done. I swallowed hard to avoid tears, but that cut deep. I still loved them, but this was the last straw. Never would I have thought it would come to this. However, it's time to live my life for me.

Rebirth begins

Chapter 20-Amira

"Amira, you must get up out this funk beautiful." Markell said as he kissed my forehead.

"I can't believe my own father said those things to me Kel. My first love has made me feel like the bottom of his shoe." I said sadly.

"Sometimes people say things they don't mean when they are upset." He tried to sugarcoat it a bit.

"He meant it. I saw it in his eyes, that's what hurts the most."

"Look, Rayna, myself and a few of my guys are going to take care of your things. I'm going bring Marlie to school and stuff as well. We'll be back later. Marcella is going to bring over lunch. We will get through this together." He said as he kissed her forehead and began walking out. I love his forehead kisses

"Kell?"

"Yeah?"

"Thanks." She said.

"It's my job! Be back later. Got to talk to you about something." He said while walking out before I can ask any questions.

He's so amazing. We are not even a couple *yet*, and he cherishes my needs like no other man has ever done. He gives me the love I longed for in a man. It took what my dad said to me to realize that I've never gotten that true father's love. It was more of a dictatorship relationship.

I finally decided to get up and take care of my hygiene. Once I was done, on cue the doorbell rang. I peeped and it was Marcella with Tupperware just like Kel said.

"Hey Marcella!!"

"Hey my bebé." She said.

"I got your favorite pasta and the rolls are fresh just like you like em!" My stomach began growling right away. She chuckled. "Looks like you are ready to eat too!"

"I am starving. Didn't realized I haven't eaten since before church on yesterday." I said.

'Hmm...Yeah, Markell told us about that."

"You don't know the half. I'm so over my parents at this point."

"I know Hun. You've got to face and fight these demons that are straying in the way of your happiness. You know that guy really cares about you."

"I know Cella. It's just….what if it's too much too soon? Are we moving too quickly? Here I am living in this beautiful home he worked so hard on…..with my client!!! "

"Chile' Love has no time frame."

"Love?"

"Yes love. No man will go out his way as he has for woman he doesn't love."

Maybe he does me love? Right?

We ate and talked for a while before she said it was time for her to head back to the restaurant.

"Don't hesitate to call me cariño, you are like a daughter to me. Okay? And let that man love you."

I nodded and hugged her. I realized it's been a couple of hours and I haven't heard from Markell or Rayna. My parents were still on reject, so I'm unsure if they have called either. I decided to call Rayna first. She finally answered sounding out of breath.

"Hello?"

"Uh Ray, please don't tell me you are having sex!" I said.

"I would have not answered your call boo, but I'm at the new spot!"

"Doing what? Wait, I have to get my things. I….."

She cut me off. "Nope. Relax. Markell and I are on it. Don't think about leaving because he took your keys. Sorry, go be lazy for a change. "

"But Rae..."

"Nothing. Bye!"

With that she hung up. Leaving me to call Markell.

"I take it you talk to Rayna huh?" He said answering is phone.

"YESS! What's going on?"

"You'll see tomorrow. I'll be back around 6 to start dinner. Marlie's eating dinner with us then she's going to Rayna's until the morning."

"Uhh okay! What am I supposed to do all day?"

"RELAX for a change! Bye baby!"

His ass hung up on me too! Oh gosh. It's going to be a long day!

After relaxing all day and binge watching Law & Order, I finally heard the door close.

"Mira!"

"Living room!"

"Hey Ms. Mira!" Marlie said happily.

"Oh, hey baby!" I said while hugging her.

"I missed you. I like your curly hair!" she said.

I washed my hair today and left it in its naturally curly state. I never really did because my mother would away say, "Lawyers should have straight hair all the time." Blah blah blah.

"Thanks honey!"

"Yeah, I like it too!" Kell said. I blushed at his compliment. "I'm going take care of dinner. Then get Marlie in her pajamas before Rayna comes."

"I can do it." I said.

"You sure?" he asked.

"Yeah, it's fine. C'mon Marlie!"

"Cominggggg" She sung.

She was so precious and full of life.

We made it to her room and she gets excited every time she walks in.

"What kind of pajamas you want to wear tonight?"

"Hmm...Princess Tiana ones!"

"Princess Tiana for Princess Marlie coming right up. With the matching socks!"

"Yayy!! Could you wash my hair and braid it for me? Daddy tries, but Grandma always has to fix it because he's not too good at it." she said causing me to giggle.

"Sure, I can do that baby!"

I went with her and assisted in her bathing time and even played dolls with her. I managed to wash her hair with some amazing shampoo I got that's suitable for me and her. I was untangling her hair and getting ready to fix her cute little pigtails that'll be sure to last the week. She has beautiful hair. She and I share the same texture, which made it easier to manage.

Chapter 21-Markell

I noticed they were up there awhile and I managed to finish dinner. It was almost time for Rayna to come and pick her up, so I decided to go check on them. I was going towards the bathroom when I noticed singing coming from Marlie's room.

"I can only give you love that lasts forever and a promise to be near each time you call
and the only heart I own, for you and you alone
that's all
that's all
I can only give you country walks in spring time
a hand to hold when leaves begin to fall
and a love whose burning light warm the winter night
that's all
that's all"

It was beautiful. The sight was even more beautiful. Amira was singing gracefully as she combed Marlie's hair. Marlie sat there combing her Barbie and repeating Amira. I didn't make my presence known yet.
"That's so pretty Ms. Mira. You sing so pretty. Did you make that song up by yourself?"

"Thank you, baby, No, that is a song by Dorothy Dandridge, I'll tell you about her one day."

"Can you be my mom Ms. Mira?"

I could tell she was taken back, hell I was too. I was about to intervene when she said something that made me love her even more.

"Uh baby, I can promise you that I am not going anywhere. I'll always be here for you like a mom if you'd like."

"Kind of like grandma?" she asked innocently

"Yes baby."

"That's great. Thanks Ms. Mira. I love you." She said.

"You love me?"

"Uhmmm...Just like daddy."

"Really?"

I took this as the moment to speak up. "Hey ladies. Food is ready and Rayna is about to be here.

"Okay daddy!" She looked in the mirror and squealed. "Oh daddy, look how pretty my hair is!!! Ohh I love it Ms. Mira! Thank you!"

She chuckled. "You are welcome baby."

Marlie left with Rayna and we ate in a comfortable silence. We kept making flirtatious stares and remarks here and there. I wanted her to know I overheard her conversation with Marlie. I also wanted her to know this made me more eager to make her officially mine.

"Mira?"

"Yes."

"I overheard you and Marlie's conversation."

"Oh I'm sorry, I just-" I cut her off.

"No. That's fine. She's never had that type of attention from anyone aside from my mom. She's never mentions her mom much, she just kinds of flow through that topic. She adores you so much and the way you treat her and responded to her made me fall more for you. I admire you as a person and even more now. Not too many take on anything with someone with as much baggage as I have."

"I adore her as well. I meant everything I said to her and I am a woman of my word. I look past any baggage you have and look at it as life lessons and blessings."

"Amira, Would to be my girlfriend. Officially?"

"Yes! Of course."

With that we shared the most passionate kissed filled with lust and now **love** as well.

Chapter 22-Amira

Markell stopped kissing me and gazed at me as he slowly slipped my shirt from my shoulders, letting it drop to the floor. He ran his hands down my arms, causing a chill to float through my body. Then he crossed our hands behind me as he kissed me long and deep, pressed so tightly against me. I let out a slight moan.

He began leaving light kisses down my neck to my collarbone causing my breath to halt a little by his touch. He smiled against my skin, knowing this was my sweet spot. I felt his hands as they unclasped my bra, He bent his head and left a trail of kisses across the tops of my breasts, his hands traveling up to cup them gently. His thumbs grazed my nipples and I almost came out of my skin. His touch alone was driving me crazy.

"Oh my" left my mouth as I dropped my head back to enjoy. His tongue flickered across my right nipple, then biting gently. I cried out, letting him know that this was exactly what I needed. His teeth nibbled more insistently and his left hand began to move toward my legs. I ran my hands up and down his back assuring him I was enjoying this.

We moved together across the room while I struggled to remove his shirt. When I took my first look at him shirtless, it was a good thing he was holding on to me so tightly, as I felt my knees shake.

He was so damn handsome and I admired his artwork on his chest. He was long and lean, strong and so sexy. He had eyes that told a story. He noticed me staring and he grinned.

"What are you staring at?"

"You. You're beautifully handsome." I ran my fingertips lightly across his chest, lower onto his stomach, and he groaned.

"Amira, you're the beautiful one in this room." he answered causing a blush to arise. "Beautiful." he breathed again, returning his hands to my body. I returned mine to his. As my fingertips slipped into the waistband of his jeans, he raised an eyebrow.

"You first." he said, scolding me lightly, reminding me of his intentions. He began walking me backward toward the couch. I knew I only had seconds left before I was going to be powerless, and I wanted him significantly more naked than he was now. I snapped open his button and unzipped them before he knew what I was doing. As his eyes widened, I slipped one hand inside, found what I was looking for, and gave him a gentle but demanding squeeze.

"Fuck, Amira . . . ," he moaned, buying me a few more seconds, which was all I needed. I slipped his jeans down his legs. He gave in, kicking off his shoes and allowing me to continue to slide them off. I knelt in front of him before he could stop me, and as I finished removing them, I chanced a quick look up. He was staring down at me with such a look of lust and want. His dark gray boxer-briefs were molded to his body as if they were made to be there. I could see his excitement underneath and my fingertips gently teased, massaging him through the fabric. His hands wound in my hair and I pressed my face against him, leaving kisses along his thighs.

I took his boxers off in a quick motion and took all of him in my mouth. No expert in this, but I guess I was doing it right.

"Oh, God Amira. Jesus," he groaned, his hands tightening in my hair, reflexively bringing him deeper into me.

I pulled back slightly, placing both hands on his length, and decided to mess with him a little. As I admired his perfection, I looked up at him with lust filled eyes. "Like this daddy?" I asked innocently, letting my tongue lick him from base to tip, playing it up as he watched me.

"Amira, what are you doing to me?" He moaned quietly, tracing his fingers lovingly around my face. And in a voice that would have made a porn star proud. Before I could say anything back. Markell had picked me up, thrown me on the couch and was now attacking me. My pants were yanked down and tossed aside. All that was left between this us was a tiny pair of black lace panties.

He tore, actually tore, my panties from my body, leaving me naked and in shock. "Oh my." Markell looked at me with lust and love in his eyes, stopping where my legs met, licking his lips. "Fucking beautiful," he groaned, and pulled my hips toward the edge of the couch, sinking down so that his face was level with them. Then he bent his head to me and began to give me the most amazing series of orgasms I had ever experienced in my entire life. When his tongue touched me, I arched off the couch so violently that he had to hold me down. "No love, you aren't going anywhere." he said.

His hands gripped my hips, angling me so that I was completely vulnerable to whatever he wished to do to me. I shivered in anticipation. "Oh, sweet Lord."

All that was heard was the sounds of our love making. It was official, I was in love with this art of a man.

Chapter 23-Amira

I woke up on a cloud; in a daze. I knew today I was going to have to put my big girl panties on. Tomorrow I had that meeting about the case and Amira Wright doesn't half ass anything.

Markell was in the bathroom and I immediately joined him.

"Morning handsome." I said to him as he brushed his teeth.

"Morning my beautiful girlfriend. Ready to start your day?" He asked.

"Ready as I'll ever be." I said nonchalantly.

"It'll be fine. I've got to run to restaurant. I'll be by your new office to bring you and Rayna lunch okay?" He asked.

"Ok babe. Love you." *Did I really say that?* He chuckled at my expression.

"Love you too. Got you donuts in the counter" We shared a kiss and he was on his way. I did my hygiene and decided on a nice blouse and dress pants for the day. I grabbed two donuts, made me coffee and was on my way to the new spot; Unsure of what to expect of course. Rayna told me she was already there waiting for me.

I made there about 15 minutes later and there were construction men. Some who I recognized as Markell's friends. They were putting up a sign, had women in a garden, men cleaning the windows. I was in total shocked, more so when I walked in.

The floors were shiny. The furniture in my old office was already in a nice glass office straight ahead which had adjustable wooden curtains. I was in total awe and it wasn't even completed yet.

"I take it you like it so far?" Rayna said.

"Oh my god. Rayna. I love it. How did you managed to get all this done in one day?" I was in disbelief.

"Well your man had a lot to do with it and of course Marco. They called some workers and they got to it. You know Marco Mexican ass cousins don't play about work. They waxed the floor, moved the stuff that belonged to you here and they began taking care of the needed construction. You just have to pick out how you want all this front area decorated and what furniture and stuff. I know you have that meeting tomorrow, so we made sure your office was done first so you can still work while the rest is under work." Rayna said.
I tried to keep my emotions together, but couldn't.

"Th- this is amazing man. Already to say it's not done. I'm so excited now. I'm so glad I got a permit already, just need to add this as the place and get inspection here once completed." I said

"Yes. I figured today we could take care of the permit stuff then go shopping for a few things." Rayna said.

"Perfect. Let me head to my new office and contact the lady. And I've got to confirm the meeting."

Chapter 24-Markell

Currently on break and work chopping it up with Marco, he asked, "Have you ever thought about getting into construction? Or even architect?"

"I've thought about. Cooking is easier to accomplish and a passion too."

"That may be true. You can do both though." He said.

"How is that?" I asked.

"Chef here part time and the other business other times." That really wasn't a bad idea. "You already have your workers. You can work there a few days and here the others. Just a suggestion. I know this place that offers the course to get your license to open such a business."

"Wow that'll be awesome. Why are you and your wife so good to us? Or any one at that." I asked.

"We had not only been blessed with the fortune due to our businesses and family pass downs, but we both were unable to have kids. Marcella could never carry a baby full term. We got checked out and it was actually both of us. Sure, we could have adopted. We just never had the chance to, the way business was booming. When we were force to move here without much to our name, people like Amira started supporting us. She began telling her colleagues and the word just continue to spread. She came along and we took a liking to her like a daughter and now you as a son."

"Wow. Thanks. Thanks a lot. Amira needs that. To someone who has lacked a true mother and daughter bond, she's amazing with Marlie."

"Some qualities come natural to people who are meant to be such." He said.

"You're right."

I went and brought lunch to Amira and ate with her for a while, then headed off to my parents' house to pick up Marlie.

"Ma!"

"Living room daddy "Marlie yelled causing me to smile.

"Hey baby girl. Hey momma." I kissed both my ladies.

"Where's daddy?" I asked.

"He went fishing with Randy from church." I nodded.

"How's Amira? Poor girl. Marlie came in boasting about her."

"She's good. Doing better already and she loves Marlie. "

Marlie wasn't paying any mind to us. We walked into the kitchen while she finished her school work and watched Disney.

"I asked her to be my girlfriend officially mom."

"I thought it was already official. That's good honey. She's a very sweet girl and plus she's Marlie approved; and we all know how Marlie can be."

"Yes. Marlie decides it all."

Before we can say anything someone began banging like police.

"What the hell?"

"Who the hell banging like this on my door?" My momma yelled.

"I want my damn child." the voice of a woman I would have never thought I'd hear. One I hated.

"Mom take Marlie upstairs. I'll handle it." I swung open the door.

"What the hell you want Tiffany? You got some nerve showing up here?"

"Oh you bad now that you got off. Heard you got that big time lawyer? How you pay for that? Mechanic job isn't that good. You hustling again?"

"None of your fucking business what the fuck I'm doing. You need to get off my porch. So my daughter and I can head home."

"Home?" She asked shocked.

"Yes home with my girl." I smirked at her, my anger not evident.

"You got another bitch playing mom to my daughter?"

"First thing. Watch your mouth. My woman ain't no bitch. Don't worry about my child. You didn't give a shit about her then. So don't worry now. I don't know what type of games you on, but watch out. Get to stepping!"

She huffed and chuckled. "You will regret dissing me. Let's see how the judge will feel that you're back hustling." With that she left in whoever car she was in.

Dumb broad. If only she knew.

"Are you okay daddy?" Marlie asked softly peaking from upstairs. I was knocked out of my rage right away when I heard my angel speak. I chucked at her innocence. "Yea baby, daddy's okay." I said.

"I heard you and her yelling."

"Huh?"

"You and my for real mommy."

I cursed at myself for being so loud and leaving the front door open.

"Daddy's sorry you heard that. Everything's okay."

"Why she doesn't love me? Did I make mommy mad? Wasn't I pretty enough."

My heart broke. No daughter should ever feel that way.

"You didn't make anyone mad baby. You are beautiful; so beautiful. I love you and that's all that matters." I kissed her.

"Grandma, grandpa, and Ms. Mira too?" She asked

I chuckled how she threw Mira in that. "Yes, all of them."

"Yayyy! Shoot! Shoot." She yelled doing this little weird dance all the kids were doing these days. I burst out laughing.

"What are you doing?" I asked.

"I'm doing the shoot dance daddy. Do it."

I was so into hitting the shoot dance with Marlie I didn't know mom had let Amira in. She immediately started dying in laughter.

"Oh, please continue." she said through laughter.

"Ha ha. Very funny." I said.

"Mommy Mira!" Marlie yelled which caused all of us to widen our eyes.

"Hey honey, how was school?" Amira asked.

"Ohh good. I drew a picture that I want you to see."

"Is that right?" Amira asked.

"Yesss!"

"Get all your things and you can show Amira at the house okay?"

"Okay daddy!" She said and then she whispered in Amira's ear. *What was that about?*

Chapter 25-Amira

I furrowed my eyebrows at what Marlie said. She said her daddy was really mad. I wonder what for. I'll make note to talk about it later.

"Telling secrets now?" He asked chuckling.

"Yep, it's a girl thing." I said jokingly.

"Oh is that right Ms. Lady??"

"That's right. Let's go so I can tell you about my day while I cook my signature dish." I said

"Ohhh. You're going to cook. Can't wait to see this."

"Don't clown, I can cook. I may not have culinary arts under my belt, but I can cook boo." I said popping my gum.

"You're funny."

Back At the House

Marlie was already washed up from by grandma. Markell was in the shower as well while I finished up dinner. I decided to my famous spaghetti with garlic bread. Very simple meal, but I heard it's both of their favorites. My mind wandered off to what Marlie mentioned to me earlier. I was wondering what Kell was upset about.

"Mmmm. Smells good in here!" He said while kissing my neck.

"Why Thanks! Just finished it up. Get Marlie while I fix the table."

"I can do that." he said.

"It's fine. Go ahead."

Marlie came zooming down. "Mm... My favorite. How did you know Momma Mira?"

"Lucky guess!" I laughed.

She giggled as she sat down.

"Very lucky guess." Markell said.

We sat and ate and they loved it.

"Daddy, can momma Mira put me to bed?" She asked.

"Uh sure. If she doesn't mind."

"Of course not, that's fine."

"Okay. I'll take care of the kitchen, then we can talk, okay?"

"Sure."

"All ready for bed baby girl?"

"Yes! Let's say our prayers now." She said.

We kneeled down and she began.

Now I lay me down to sleep.
I pray the Lord my soul to keep.
If I should die before I wake,
I pray to God my soul to take.
If I should live for other days,
I pray the Lord to guide my ways.
Dear God,
Thank you for Daddy, Maw maw, Paw paw, and Ms. Mira.
Could you make Ms. Mira my new mommy for good? Thank you and Amen"

She'd just warmed my heart. "Amen. "I said.

I kissed her forehead and tucked her in. She has definitely stolen my heart. She's the sweetest little thing.

"Hey you! "I said as I straddled Kel's lap.

"Hey pretty lady. How'd the tuck in session go?"

"Good. She's precious!"

He chuckled. "Thanks, she's something. I'm sorry if she's being a little forward."

"Oh no. It's fine. I love her. She makes me feel loved and wanted."

"Good. How was your day? "He asked.

"GREAT! The place looks awesome and we got so much done. Inspection is in three weeks."

"That's more than enough time to finish everything off. I wanted to talk to you about what Marco and I talked about."

"Okay, what's that?"

"He mentioned to me about opening a business with construction or architect in addition to being co chef part time."

"Wow. That'll be great. Doing what you love together. That would be awesome. I'm here to support you."

"Yeah, I'm going to look into that. He was going to take me see a friend of his next week. Everything set for that meeting?"

I sighed heavily. "Yeah, ready as I'll ever be. I hope we can get this in a bag. I'm glad you are clear, but this shit is still in the air and I hate it. Speaking, of Marlie mentioned you were upset earlier, what for?"

I can see him clenching his jaw at that statement. "Yes, I was pissed. Her mom decided to stop by."

I shifted a bit and sat beside him. We never really talked much about Marlie's mom, so I really don't know where all that stands to be sure.

"What did she have to say?"

"It's what she didn't say. How she's going to tell the judge I'm hustling again if I don't let her see her child and all kind of stupid shit. Which leads me more to the reason that she may have been the one to set me up."

"Oh wow. I know we talked briefly about why she's not in Marlie's life, but we never really talked it out in full."

He sighed and rubbed his chin like he was in deep thought. "I met Tiffany at the club while I was hustling. I was well known for what I did and because I had money. I was about 19 and was running the streets. I attracted a lot of women, aside from what I looked like but because I had money. I noticed Tiffany a few times, but I never paid her much mind. One night, she approached me. I gave her conversation and we start kicking it. I developed feelings for her and everything. I would wine and dine her, had her living the life in a Condo downtown. Hell, I thought I was in love. That went on for about two years. I went to surprise her one night when I was done with working early and she was riding another nigga's dick; not just any nigga either, my first cousin. Of course, I dead that situation. About a month later, she came to me saying she was pregnant. Of course I knew I was a possibility, but hell, anybody could have been it. I handle my side a bit until she was born and got the DNA test done. It came back that Marlie was mine, and I never left since. I was there every day for Marlie. I fell in love all over again with Marlie. I stayed every night in the house with Marlie. I did my dirt, but I made sure I was back for Marlie. I wasn't paying much mind to Tiff because my focus was on Marlie.

After about 3 months, I decided to give it a chance for Marlie's sake. WRONG CHOICE! She was so jealous of the attention I gave Marlie. She felt like she had to compete against her own daughter. It was silly. One night I came back, niggas was all in the living room, Marlie was crying in her crib, her momma was giving niggas dome in the room. I flipped the fuck out!! I knew after that; Tiff was going to try some shit. I had a feeling. No sooner than that, the police was raiding everything I own and arrested me in the process. Marlie was in my mom's custody. I was sentenced to 7 years, but with all the shit I was doing in there, I got out after only doing 2 1/2. I fought for custody of Marlie and got it completely. We moved in with my parents for good and we been connected at the hip ever since. I never talk to Tiffany, she never tried to fight for custody, and she wasn't in our lives. Her parents tried to fight me once I was released, but that was it. So I was pissed she decided to stop by today."

"Wow. I'm sorry baby." I said.

"It's all good. Got another blessing as a result."

"What's that?"

"You Amira Wright!" I blushed.

He's something I tell you.

Chapter 26-Amira

Next Day; the Meeting.

I woke up bright and early and was ready for this meeting. After what Markell told me last night, I knew I had to be on my A game in case she tried anything. After a long debate, he agreed to put a report for disturbance or her, his mom did the same. I made him do that just in case, so they will know that she was picking for trouble. That way, I'll have the documents to prove it.

Kel and Marlie were already gone for the day. I headed to Starbucks since it's been awhile since I've stopped.

"Good morning, Welcome to Starbucks!"

"Morning, Can I have a Grande Vanilla Latte please with an extra shot of espresso and a Ham & Cheddar Artisan Breakfast Sandwich?"

"Sure. That'll be $8.00. Drive around please."

I did just that and the lady smiled when she noticed it was me. "Well hello, you haven't been by in a while."

"I know, changed up my routine a bit." I said while handing her the money.

"Understandable. Here's your order. Have a great day!" She said while giving me change.

"Same to you. Thanks!"

I made it to the meeting 30 minutes early, which was awesome of course. I called Rayna and she made sure everything was set at the office. She was on her way in case I needed her.

I finished off my breakfast, popped a mint then gum in. I made sure my lipstick was just right. I was naturally beautiful today. I went easy on the makeup with a nice coral Blazer and pant suit.

To my surprise, Judge McCain was the judge which is a plus because he adores me.

"Good morning Judge!"

"Ahh Good morning Ms. Wright, Pleasure to see you again."

"Likewise, sir."

"And you are early as always."

"Yes sir, if you are right on time, then you are too late."

"That is correct."

On cue, Roger came in with a woman, who I assumed to be his assistant. Rayna came following. Everyone greeted and we got this show on the road.

"Okay Ms. Wright, We have proved that your client was indeed not responsible for what he was charged with which caused those charges to be dropped. Now we are trying to find out who exactly did this correct?" Judge asked

"Yes your honor."

"Very well then. Proceed."

"Well sir, I have a reason to believe his child's mother could be responsible, or may know of someone who is."

"Funny that you mentioned it, here is my client that you are speaking of, Tiffany Granger."

I swallowed. Not because I'm scared, because I'm now facing the woman who once had my man's heart and broke it of course. Not only that, I wasn't aware that clients were attending the meeting.

"Nice to meet you. Wasn't aware clients were going to be in attendance of the meeting. I would have included mine."

"Where is Mr. Davis?" Judge asked.

"Currently at work sir."

"Does he still have the chef job?"

"Yes sir." I smirked once I noticed the shock on Tiffany's face.

"Very well then. Rogers's better communication should have been made, but we shall proceed because I'm sure you have a valid reasoning for her being here."

"Yes you honor I do. My new client has come to me that Mr. Davis is back to selling drugs due to him no longer living with his parents." I laughed to myself at this.

"Do you have evidence for such?"

"No, but-"

"No evidence sir. Rogers you have been in this line of work to know how this process works."

"I have evidence that Ms. Granger went to Mr. Davis' parents' home and caused a disturbance. Here are the police reports from both my client his mother. Here is also his legal address, with his name and form of payment which equals to the money made from his mechanic shop over the years, his advance from his current employer, and his salaried pay. Everything he owns is legally and rightfully his." I stated matter factually. The judge and Rogers reviewed it. I could notice Tiffany growing uncomfortable.

"Very well then. Get officers in here please."

Tiffany looked scared. I didn't know why he was calling them in. Once one of them came he whispered something in their ear. In a matter of 10 minutes they were back with papers and they whispered in his ear, this time not leaving the room.

"I've reviewed all of these documents. Although I can't prove it just yet and it must go to trial about you being involved in this case Ms. Granger, you have outstanding warrants for your arrest for theft and driving without a license." Judge McCain said.

She got teary eyed and Rogers looked upset. How you don't do research on your clients, big dummy. He wants to beat me so bad until he's stupid.

"You have the right to remain silent. Anything you say will be used against you in a court of law. You have the right to an attorney during interrogation; if you cannot afford an attorney, one will be appointed to you." The officer said.

She began sobbing. "This isn't fair."

I wanted to say what's not fair is Marlie not having her mother, but I opted out and decided to keep it professional.

We finished this meeting off and they will contact me on trial. I can't believe how that went. Wait until I tell Markell this!

"Afternoon Marcella." I said making my presence known.

"Afternoon baby. How are you?" She asked

"Pretty good. How are you?"

"Well. Just finished that lunchtime rush. Markell should be on lunch shortly. Want to order something while you wait?"

"Yes ma'am. I want the barbecue chicken with roasted potatoes and a sweet tea please." I said.

"Sure. Coming right up darling. Malaina, the new waitress will get your sweet tea."

I nodded and thanked her.

"Hey beautiful." Markell said walking in looking handsome as ever.

He came over and hugged and kissed me like he missed me.

"Mm someone missed me." I said.

He bit his lip and said "You just don't know. That skirt you have on isn't helping either."

Just the sound of his voice brings a waterfall between my thighs. However, I really wanted to talk to him about this meeting and his baby momma making an appearance. I began to explain everything and he was baffled.

"What the hell man! Who did you say her attorney was? "

"Rogers. I think his first name is Mark. I always addressed him by his last name."

"That lowlife bastard."

I furrowed my eyebrows.

"You know him?"

He chuckled. "Use to roll the streets with him. He was a big dealer and also a man I thought I could trust. He was too damn jealous though. I caught him fucking Tiffany."

"Oh my God. He's the one?"

"Yep. Bitch ass nigga still jealous."

"So this is a personal vendetta for him behind you, aside from me?"

"What you mean?" He asked.

"He attempted to get with me and I dissed him in front of some pretty big people and he's been pissed at me ever since. I don't give a shit though."

"This shit crazy and I have a feeling this isn't over with."

Chapter 27-Amira

"Amira Wright speaking." I said as I answered my phone.

"Hi, it's Detective Jones. I was calling about your office and home?"

"Home, I'm currently at home."

"You no longer reside at 4122 Rochester Ave?"

"No sir, what happened?"

"Well the home was vandalized as well at hateful words on the property at Wright and Curtis law firm. Your father is on his way here, but being it was towards you we have to ask you some questions."

"Towards me? And I no longer work there either. "

"Yes ma'am. Please stop by the station."

I couldn't believe this. I'm wondering will I ever get a break. This is too much.

"Babe, I should come with you." Markell said.

"You don't have to. You know my dad."

"All due respect, I don't give a damn about your dad. Let's go!"

I didn't dare protest. We headed to the station. Thankfully Marlie was with her grandparents.

We arrived to the station a few minutes later. My parents were sitting there unbothered. I noticed how my dad clenched his jaw when he noticed Markell was right in tow with me.

"Ms. Wright? Thanks for coming down. I'm Detective Johnson." he said shaking my head.

"Hi, and this is my boyfriend Markell." I said proudly and loudly enough for my parents to hear. My mom scoffed, but I honestly could care less.

We followed the detective. My parents started to follow, but the detective stopped them.

"Just your daughter and her boyfriend. We've asked all the questions we need for now. If we need anything else, we will call you all." He told him.

My dad didn't look too happy with that, but they reluctantly left. Not before looking my way with disgust. I shook it off and continued to follow the detective.

"Have a seat guys. I noticed the tension. Not good with the parents right now? "He asked.

"No, because I refuse to live the life they want me to live."

He nodded writing something down.

"Do you have any idea who would do this?"

I sighed. "I know Attorney Rogers have this personal vendetta against me, but I don't know. And well, his ex." I said gesturing towards Markell who is very uneasy in this station.

"What about your parents?" He asked.

"I mean they are something and has gone far as putting my home for sale, but vandalism on their own things?" I asked.

"Possible." Markell said.

The detective said he would call us if he needed or heard something.

We rode back in an eerie silence; I guess trying to make sense of all of this. I know my parents and I had bad blood, but would they go that far behind Markell?

"Mira, I know you don't want to think that your parents would stoop that low, but you can deny that it's possible."

"Maybe so? But that's his office. His home." I said trying to convince myself.

"Yes it is, but it could be to throw off the possibility of them. Look, I'm not trying to put you against your parents although they are against you. I'm just saying. "

"Just as your ex is a possibility as well." I said.

"And that's true!"

Omniscient

Amira's father made it to the warehouse not long after leaving the station.

"This is wrong." Amira's mother said.

"Just shut up. I'm really not up for the nagging today because you're just as wrong as I am." He said while slamming the door leaving her the car alone.

She started sobbing immediately "Oh gosh." She said.

Meanwhile, he made it inside.

"You got my money?" the person asked

"Yes, it's all there. Make sure you handle your part of the deal."

"Yeah yeah."

Chapter 28-Markell

I took off today and decided to stop by my Aunt Celeste's house. Her house was the spot. The hood respected her like a mother. Her son was my partner in crime. He always wanted to take the fall for me, but I'd never allow him. Unfortunately, he just can't leave that life alone.

"Hey nanny." I said walking in.

"Oh hey baby. Good to see you." We talked for a while before I went out back.

"Was sup fools?" I greeted my cousin Dylan and his boys.

"Was sup pretty boy. You finally came to holla. That girl got you open huh?" He said jokingly.

"Whatever, but check this...ya'll heard anything about some people vandalizing an office and house.

"Yeah. Ro & his niggas."

"Ro?? As in Rogers?" I asked.

"Yes. The nigga a lawyer now too." my cousin said.

"Yeah, that's the nigga who tried to get me down. He also baby mom's lawyer too."

"Word? That dude still on that same shit. We gon check it out and let you know. I really want to knock his head off, but I know you want to know the details first Mr. Changed man."

"Yeah, keep me posted. I got to go man, I got a daughter and woman now"

"Woman? She must be special for you to be claiming her and Marlie in the same sentence." Dylan joked.

"Yes, she's wifey man. Marlie been calling her mom and all that."

"That's was sup. Marls need a stable motherly figure."

"I'm going to see what I can find out. Come back later on okay, I will have something. If I hear something before you come back, I'll call ya" Dylan said.

"Bet!" We dapped up and I headed to the restaurant for a bit.

Dylan finally called me saying he had some information. I told him to come over and it was only right for Mira be here too.

"Damn, you really finished this up. It's nice cuz. "

"Thanks man! When you're ready we can work together with this construction"
"I'll sleep on it."

On cue, Mira made it home. "Babe!" She yelled.

"In the den!"

"Oh hey, didn't know we had company."

"This my cousin Dylan I told you about. Dylan this my baby Amira."

"Nice to finally meet you love, but to the reason I'm here. Rogers has been meeting up with some old' school cat, last name Wright. He forever investing money into Ro's schemes; for years."

Amira's face and heart dropped. She couldn't believe it. "Oh my God"

"You okay?" Dylan asked.

"That's her dad man." I said.

"Oh shit. That's not it. Seems like your father owe some bad people money. He may also know your baby moms on a different level fam"

"What you mean D??"

He sighed. "He sleeping with her man. Been knockin' her off obviously. Since uh..."

"Uh what"

"Before Marlie" he mumbled.

"Whatttttttttttttt" Mira and I yelled.

I was pissed to say the least.

"D, let's ride.'"

I was going get some answers out that bitch!

"Where are you going?" She asked through tears.

"Just to see about Marlie, I'll be back." Kissed her and walked out before she could say anything else.

Chapter 29-Markell

"You ready to go in cuz?" Dylan asked

"Yeah, this dumb broad going to give me some answers."

I banged on the door. "Tiffany, Open the damn door!!!"

She finally opened with a terrified look on her face. I got all in her face. "What type of games you playing? You fucking old men now? Is Marlie mine? Is she?" I screamed and banged against the wall above her head causing pictures to fall off the wall.

"Stop screaming!" She yelled through tears.

"Look Tiff, tell the man what he wants."

"I don't know Markell!!! I don't know!!"

"You dumb Bitch!!! I love that lil girl with everything in me, every damn fiber of my body and you going to tell me now after all this time that she may not be mine?! You lucky I don't hit women!! Who may be the other dad Tiffany?"

"Wright."

"You got to be shitting me bruh?" So you in on their lil plan huh? Tiffany you know what I am capable of and you want to test me."

"Please Markell, I'll do anything."

"Now you want to do the right thing? Tell the truth for once. This is not over Tiffany, not by a long shot!!!"

With that, I stormed out. If I stayed any longer, I'll hit her and I don't hit women.

"You sure you don't want me to handle that cuz?" Dylan asked.

"Nah. I got it."

I was sitting in my car contemplating. I did a DNA Test for Marlie, so do I need another one? A million and one thoughts were going through my head.

Chapter 30-Amira

We were riding around everywhere trying to find Kel. He was not answering his phone and it was driving me insane. I was growing more and more pissed. I decided that it was time I let my parents really have it. This was getting insane.

"Ray, let's go to my parents' house."

"Mira are you sure?"

"I am positive."

"Well you know I'm always down to ride."

A few minutes later we made it to my parents' house. It was about dinner time, so I noticed my siblings were all here. I also noticed another car that I didn't recognize. I didn't care who was here. As long as they were here, I was letting it all out. I am sick of these people. I didn't even bother to ring the doorbell or knock, I used my old spare key and walked right in. They were all smiling and laughing and who was sitting at their table along with them? Rogers.

"If this isn't some shit!" Rayna said.

"Well hello family!" I said sarcastically.

They all looked like they seen a ghost. At the same time, Markell was calling me back. I gave the phone to Rayna.

"We at her parents' house and uh it is not looking good." Rayna said to him.

"H-hey baby" My mother stuttered.

"Save it mama!" She looked taken back.

"Look Mira." Aniya, my sister tried to speak up.

"You shut up you too!!" I yelled.

"Nice to see you here Rogers. I see you and my father still doing business deals." The two of them looked at me with widen eyes

"Yeah, I know about all of your crooked shit daddy."

"Now you will watch your language when speaking to me, I am still your father."

"Are you now? Shouldn't a man who is respectful to others get respect in return. You are a liar and a deceiver."

"Amira!" My mother yelled.

"No momma, I am not finished."

"Tell her daddy, tell her everything. I know she may know some of your dirt, but I'm sure she doesn't know all of it."

"Amira, you are on thin ice!! I suggest you stop while you are ahead." My father said.

"Oh I am just getting started Dad. Tell momma how you were sleeping with Roger's client, who happens to be my boyfriend's baby mother. Oh, also tell mom how you may be her child's father. Tell her that dammit!" I yelled.

He slapped me causing me to stumble, but out of nowhere Markell appeared and punched my dad in his jaw. Rogers tried to get up and leave without being seen, but Markell caught him and knock him out completely causing both of my sister's husband to say "DAMMMNN!"

I finally regained myself. My dad was sitting with an ice pack on his jaw. Rayna took Markell outside.

"You are a poor excuse of a man. Poor excuse! You drop this thing you and Rogers got planned or I will make your life a living hell. You have ruined me for many years and I will not go for it much longer. I will not! That man out there has showed the love that I wanted from you. Now he has to deal with the fact that my own father may be his daughter's biological father. You are twisted and will pay for what you've done!!! "I said through tears.

"Amira!" Aniya and Amaya yelled.

"WHAT!"

"Don't leave like this..."

"I'm over this family! I'm over it. It's too toxic."

Meanwhile Amira's mom was packing her bags for a hotel stay.

"Where the hell you think you are going?" Amira's dad asked.

"Away from you. This has gone too far. I stuck by your side through it all and you possibly made a whole child on me? I went along with your scheme to remove Markell from her life, but he isn't the toxic person you are. You were afraid your dirty laundry would air from the jump, this is why you did not want to take on his case and this is why you forbid his relationship with Amira! I hate you!!"

With that, she stormed out. Amira, Markell, and Rayna were leaving. She and Amira made eye contact; she stared at her daughter with tear filled regretful eyes and mouthed,

"I'm so sorry."

Amira's father was in his bedroom making a mess. His world was finally crumbling down.

Chapter 31-Markell

I really tried my best to contain my anger for Amira because I know at the end of the day; he will always be her father. However, seeing him putting his hands on her did something to me. That really did it for me. I was raised to NEVER put my hands on a woman, regardless of the circumstances. At that point, I didn't care who he was.

Dylan and I were headed to the house behind Amira and Rayna. Thank God we had the two of them with us because neither of us was in the position to drive. We both were upset. I was so hurt and lost. I am just trying to put all the pieces together. Marlie is my world. She is the reasoning behind everything I do.

"Cuz, nothing changes. You know that right?" Dylan stated breaking me out of my thoughts.

"I know cuz. This is just breaking me down. I mean. I did a DNA test."

"Yea and DNA don't lie. However, Amira pops probably got pull somewhere. Need to explore all options. Regardless though, that's your daughter. There's no changing that. Oh, and Amira is a real one."

"Yea, she is. I know this is tearing her apart. She worship the ground that dude walked on, their entire family did. She just doesn't know the kind of person he really is." I thought about how she didn't even know how their entire livelihood was funded through her father's mischief.

We arrived at the house and all exit the vehicles in complete silence. No words were said, all we heard was the wind as we walked to the door. She must've given her keys to Rayna, she opened the door.

As soon as we walked in Amira tried to get to moving fast. I noticed that whenever she is worried or upset, she tried to drown herself in a task to avoid facing it. Clearly that was her answer all these years.

"Okay guys. I'll get something started so you all could eat. I know you all are hungry. What do you-?"

I cut her off immediately

"Wait a minute. You don't have to cook anything. We are fine." I told her.

"Yea boo. We are good. We are going to hang around for a bit. You two go ahead and talk. We'll be fine. "Rayna assured.

She reluctantly followed me upstairs into the master bedroom. We sat in total silence for a few minutes before I decided to speak up.

"Amira, I know a lot has transpired. We don't have to talk about it all right now. However, we need to talk about it." I said.

"You know I was worried that you were getting yourself in trouble. We were looking all over for you. Did you go by Tiffany's?" She asked.

"Yes. Dylan and I went by there. I won't lie and say that I had a mind frame to cause havoc once I arrived, but I thought about Marlie. I thought about you as well." I said honestly.

"Me?" She asked.

"Yes. You. I knew I had too much to lose. I'm so seriously on living a better life. Tiffany know how to hit me where it hurts. She knows my daughter is my everything. She is weakness. "I said getting emotional.

Chapter 32-Amira

Markell started getting emotional which in turned caused me to get emotional. He was not the one to show emotion like that, so I know that this was a lot for him. I was emotional with everything, but I know his pain was different.

I saw how he was with his daughter. I mean even the bond we created was special. I can begin to imagine her being my baby sister. Just the thought alone makes my skin crawl. I walked over to where he sat on the edge of the bed and just held him as he cried.

"We are going to get through this together." I said softly.

"Mira, your dad really isn't all he claimed to be." He said.

"Yes. I know that now." I said.

"He gambled with some pretty serious people in the streets. He borrowed the money that he used to open his practice. He was able to continue everything because he got a lot of people in high places in the gambling scheme as well."

"So he just had some big old scheme going on." That was when it hit me. There were times when he swore he had to stay late for cases. He and my mom would argue about this all the time. Of course I assumed things, but I never spoke it. I didn't think he would ever stoop that low.

"See, to avoid him paying his debt, he got other people involved. He never had to pay. I guess somewhere in the mix he met Tiffany. Her brothers are into that mess.

It's just so weird how I worlds collided though." He said out loud, but more to himself.

"Markell, you know that I would never hurt you right? I've been nothing, but really with you. Our worlds colliding is nothing, but coincidence" I said just in case even had any thoughts.

"Amira, I know that. One thing I've learned dealing with Tiffany or any one in my past is how to read people. When someone shows you their true intentions, believe them. You've showed me who you are in such a short period of time. I am not questioning you; this is just some crazy shit." He chuckled.

"Yea, it really is. So, about Marlie. You really think you need to get another DNA test?"

"To be honest, it would only be for knowledge because that's my baby girl. There's no changing that."

I wouldn't lie and say that I didn't want to know myself.

"I could arrange for someone to come by the office. I mean that's if you want to know."

"Yea, that's cool. What's next with the case?"

"Oh gosh. I forgot that I had a message from the lead detective on the case. So much has happened today that it slipped my mind to give him a call back."

Before I get a chance to do that, Rayna came running upstairs with my phone.

"Amira, your sister is on the phone screaming! You know I only deal with any of them because of you. I won't be dealing with all that. Here!" She stated handing me the phone.

"Really Amira? You will have your own father arrested? "My sister yelled crying.

"Aniya, what are you even talking about?"

"What am I talking about? It's mighty funny that after the scene you just caused the cops came here to arrest daddy for arson. That's your daddy Amira!" She yelled before hanging up.

"What the hell…"

Chapter 33-Amira

I woke stating that today would be a new day.

I woke up saying that I controlled my life and what happens with it.

My dad was indeed arrested that night, exactly one month ago today.
Today was also the conclusion date of his trial. Yep, his trial. It turns out that even though at the time he was able to post bail, it was later revoked.

My dad's rap sheet suddenly grew over night. He was being charged with embezzlement and racketeering to be exact also accessory to arson. My entire family was the center of every news station.

Talk about embarrassment. So of course, the entire Wright & Curtis staff had to undergo investigation, me included. It was all a part of the procedure. My new firm was fully investigated for legitimacy as well. Our entire lives were under scrutiny behind my father's greed. My sisters were finally seeing our family were not as perfect as we pretended to be all these years. Growing up, we never had sisterly relationships because we were too busy competing against one another trying to be what our father wanted us to be. As for my mom, I blamed her for being blinded by love. My dad was at least smart enough to keep some of his dirt away from her. As upset as I was at her too for turning a blind eye, I didn't want her to pay for his mistakes. I didn't want my mom to go to prison.

"You ready to walk in boo?" Markell asked.

I gave him a small smile and nodded. He's been by my side through this whole process. Even with dealing with his personal mishaps and feelings. The DNA test results came in on yesterday. He didn't open them yet. I'm not quite sure if he even cares to do so. Marlie is his. There's no changing that.

"Yes, let's head on in. I know the cameras are going to be ready."

The minute we step foot outside, cameras and reporters were all over.
With my dad being one of the top earning attorneys and our entire family being attorneys, this is what came with the territory. I walked in with my head held high though because I earned everything I have.

"ALL RISE! This court is now in session. The honorable Judge Lansford presiding."

We sat through the entire process of hearing all the charges, the witnesses that I didn't know exist, business and families affected. It was heartbreaking to say the least. My sisters and I may not be as close as we should, but this have brought us closer.

We all sat quietly awaiting the verdict. My mother as well. She and I hadn't really talked much since the trial began, but I gave her hand a squeeze. She looked up and gently squeeze back.

"We, the jury, find the defendant, Randal Wright, to be guilty of the charges of embezzlement and racketeering."

My mother burst out into tears. My sisters cried silently while I just sat there without any emotions. Not that I wasn't hurt because I was. I was embarrassed and even felt betrayed. This man taught me about law. I found the love for it through his teachings. Granted he didn't always show me fatherly love and it was more of a dictatorship, it still hurt.

However, as well as I knew the law. I knew that he must pay for the consequences of his actions. That I knew.

As we walked out the court room a reporter walked up to me. Markell attempted to stop them, but I gently removed his hand.

"Ms. Amira, How do you think this will affect your career as an attorney? Where will you go from here?" She asked.

"This only motivates me to continue to fight for what's right. This only showed me that I still have more things to learn. I will go forward from here. I worked hard to become an attorney. It took many long days and nights. I EARNED my rights to be an attorney and nothing will change that." I said proudly as we walked to our vehicles.

Chapter 34-Markell

Things have been extremely crazy lately. So crazy that I haven't taken the time to read these DNA results. Maybe I was afraid on what it may say. I know it doesn't change anything, but still. It's hurts to even imagine that she may not be biologically mine.

"Looking at it won't make it go away babe." Amira stated. She was standing there looking so peaceful. I don't if she was finally feeling free or what, but she looked great. In spite all that has been going on.

"Yea. I guess we need to get it over with."
She did the honors of opening the results. She read it and started crying. I did too. I just knew it.

"You are her biological father Kel." She said through tears.

"Seriously?" I asked softly

"YESSSS" She said excitedly as she kissed me.

"THANK GOD!" I said through tears.
I ran into her room and grabbed her tightly kissing her all over her face.

"Daddyyyyyyyy.... I'm trying to watch Princess and the frog" She whined trying to move me out the way.

I couldn't help, but smile. That's my baby right there. There's no changing that.

"I'm sorry baby. Daddy just wanted to show you some love. Love you baby girl."

"Love you daddy." She said without looking, causing me to chuckle.

Epilogue-Amira
ONE YEAR LATER

"Amira, don't forget you have a scheduled lunch with the mayor tomorrow at 2." Rayna voiced.

"I won't. She is scheduled right after my interview with Channel 10 news. I remembered everything. I'm heading out though. My family is waiting for me." I smiled.

"Oh, how can I forget? It's Monday's dinner." She joked.

"I'll see you shortly silly." I laughed.

Yes, that's right. Monday night dinners are still at thing, but they are held at my home with my family. Yes, my entire family.

My mom, sisters, Rayna, my god baby, Marco and his wife, oh and My HUSBAND and KIDS of course. Life has a way of hitting you in many ways unexpectedly. Some things serve as lessons and blessings. I'm grateful for my blessings. My family is stronger and better than ever now. I also found out why I was glowing so much, I was pregnant!

I gave birth to a beautiful baby girl. She and Marlie are my everything. Not to mention, once I found out we were expecting Markell asked me to marry him.

Speaking of, His business has been booming. Yep, he started that architect business. He still helps at Marco's when he can as well. He is truly doing what he loves and I'm so proud of him.

Let's just said this is what happened when I stumbled across an unlikely love. I finally found the solace that I desperately needed, on my own terms.

THE END

Author's Note:

What a ride!

I truly hope you enjoyed this story. It was book one of my "Strength of a Woman Series". I chose that as the theme of my series because I wanted to truly touch on women finding their strength, regardless of the situation. Amira really had to find her own way. She had to show that she was fully capable of making her own decisions and still be successful.
Oh, and Markell…
He just couldn't get a break huh. It's crazy how people try to use your past life against you. He truly showed the people he wasn't what he used to be. He did what he had to do for his baby girl and for himself.
Markell & Amira truly balance each other out and I'm glad they found their Happily Ever After!

If you enjoyed this, please Stay Tuned for the next book up in the series, COMING REAL SOON!

Follow me at @KiaraJonai on all platforms to stay up to date.

CPSIA information can be obtained
at www.ICGtesting.com
Printed in the USA
LVHW031656290120
645190LV00005B/586

9 781674 950945